RULES OF THE HEART

HEARTS MEDICAL SERIES BOOK 1

EMILY HAYES

1

ELLA

"Wendy? What are you doing?"

Wendy turned to Dr. Ella Ashton, her face blotchy with tears. "I'm leaving."

"What are you talking about? You can't leave! We've got your surgery scheduled for tomorrow."

Wendy took a shuddering breath. "My insurance just called. They won't pay for it."

"But... But you need the surgery. I wrote them a letter explaining it. The only way to cure the cancer is to cut it out of your brain."

"They say the procedure is too experimental. They won't cover it."

Ella wanted to scream. Yes, this type of tumor

extraction wasn't mainstream yet, but it had been done half a dozen times in different places all over the world. She hadn't done one herself yet, but she had watched every video and spent hours reading up on the theory. She knew she could do it.

"Let me talk to them. There has to be a way to work this out. Don't leave just yet."

Wendy's eyes lit up with hope. "You really think there's a way we can figure it out?"

She knew this surgery was her last chance. If she didn't have it, she would be dead within a month.

"I'll figure something out, I promise."

Wendy stepped forward and wrapped her arms around Ella. "Thank you, Doctor Ashton. I don't know what I'd do without you."

"Don't you worry, Wendy. I'm sure the insurance people can be reasonable."

Five hours, seven phone calls and two screaming matches later, it turned out that the insurance people could not, in fact, be reasonable. Ella was fairly sure she had fractured something in her foot from kicking a wall in frustration. No matter which way she put it, Wendy's insurance simply would not pay for the life-saving surgery Wendy needed.

The thought of going back to Wendy and telling her that she was going to die in a month was unbearable. There had to be something else she could do.

She shoved her phone angrily into her pocket and marched up to James' office. James was the Head of Surgery. Surely, he could help her.

"Ella, come in." James greeted her with a friendly smile. The knot in Ella's chest loosened slightly. James wasn't like the insurance people, just out to make money. He had become the Head of Surgery because he wanted to help people. Surely, he could be reasonable.

"I need permission to do a surgery pro-bono."

The smile slid off James' face to be replaced with a cautious expression. "Which surgery?"

"It's the one for Wendy Anderson, to remove her brain tumor."

"Ella, that's a very expensive surgery."

"Which is exactly why it needs to be pro-bono. She can't afford it and her insurance won't pay for it."

"I'm sorry, Ella, but the hospital is already at capacity for pro-bono surgeries. We simply can't afford to take on any more."

"WHAT? How can you say that! She's only

nineteen, James! She has no one. Her parents disowned her when she was eighteen, when she came out as gay. She was diagnosed with an inoperable tumor a few months later and has been fighting ever since. She *needs* this surgery, James! She will be dead very soon if we don't help her."

"Don't you raise your voice to me, Ella. I understand the situation, and it's not that I don't have sympathy, but I need to look at the big picture here. The hospital needs to stay in business if we're to help anyone, and if we want to stay in business, we can't just go handing out pro-bono surgeries to anyone who asks."

"It's not anyone," Ella said through gritted teeth. "I'm asking. Consider it a personal favor. Please, James. Wendy needs this. *I* need this."

"Like you needed the last one? That homeless refugee woman? Or the vet who was turned away by the VA? Do you realize that seventy percent of the pro-bono surgeries for the year have gone to you?"

Ella felt a flicker of guilt, wondering how many other doctors had been turned down because of her, but when she thought of the patients she had saved, she couldn't feel truly guilty for long.

"Then borrow from next year's pro-bono surgeries. It's only two months away. Wendy can't wait two months, though."

"It doesn't work like that. I'm sorry, Ella, but that's my final word."

Ella turned and stormed out, slamming the door behind her. What kind of fucked-up world was this where people put profit above lives?

Well, she wasn't going to stand for it. James may not be on her side, but she knew people who would be. She only needed one fellow neuro surgeon, a resident, an intern and two surgical nurses. She would prefer a full team, but she could make do with those five.

Ella went through names in her head, wondering who would be most willing to break the rules with her. She would need to get at least two or three extra nurses on board, of course, to cover up the absence of five staff members should James question their absence.

Ella spent the rest of the day in clandestine negotiations. She called in every favor she was owed and made promises that were going to be hell to keep, but she would do it. What was a month of doing a resident's charts when Wendy could have her whole life ahead of her?

The sun was setting by the time Ella returned to Wendy's room.

"You were turned down, weren't you?" Wendy's eyes were dull and lifeless, like she had given up already. "I heard you shouting earlier."

"One way or another, you are getting the surgery," Ella growled. "We can do it, but we have to do it right now. Are you ready?"

"What? But I thought they turned you down?"

"It's a long story and we don't have a lot of time. We need to do this at the change of shift if we're going to—look, I'll explain it afterward. Do you still want the surgery?"

"I—of course! Yes. I'll do whatever you need me to do."

"All you need to do is lie back and let us do the work. You've fought this cancer for months. Now, it's my turn."

Ella wheeled Wendy's bed down to surgery herself while one of the nurses kept watch. Everyone snuck into the OR one at a time, scrubbing quickly and stepping into the main room while glancing back over their shoulders, clearly worried about being caught.

"Alright, everyone. I know we're all anxious about what'll happen if anyone finds out we're missing, but we can't focus on that now, not if we're going to help Wendy. We need to concentrate on doing our jobs. If this goes south, I will take full responsibility for it. For now, just think about what you need to do. We can deal with all the rest later."

There were murmurs of agreement through the room. Ella looked down at Wendy. "Are you ready?"

"I'm ready, Doctor Ashton."

"Then count backward from ten."

Wendy got to seven before she was out like a light. Ella took the scalpel that one of the nurses handed to her.

From that moment onward, she was in her zone. When she was doing a surgery, nothing else mattered. It was just her and the scalpel and the brain in front of her.

Ella went over everything she had learned in her head, applying the techniques to Wendy's brain.

There it was—the tumor. Now, she just needed to extract it without destroying any of the surrounding tissue. She had planned this surgery with great care. She could do it, she was sure she could do it.

Ella fought the urge to hold her breath. It was

an urge she still had, even though she had defeated it as an intern. She breathed slowly and steadily as she used her scalpel to work carefully around the tumor, going under the main brain stem.

Tumors like Wendy's were usually considered inoperable, but with this new technique of using cameras to cut under the brain stem without cutting into the stem itself, Ella should be able to excise the tumor.

Should being the operative word.

Just a little bit more... There. Ella plucked the tumor out and examined the surrounding brain. She couldn't see any damage, but that didn't mean much.

"Alright, the tumor is out. It's time to run the scan."

The scan was a new development that the hospital had spent a fortune on, at Ella's insistence. It allowed them to scan for damage to specific brain functions before closing a patient up. This way, they would be able to tell now whether or not Ella had messed up, and if she had, she still had a chance to fix it.

Ella may not be holding her breath, but everyone else in the ER was. She attached the probes to Wendy's brain and turned on the scanner. One by one, lights started to flash. Green. Green. Green. Not a single splash of red that would indicate damaged functions. Green and more green.

When the last light flicked to green, everyone cheered, Ella included.

"Alright, people, good job! Let's close her up and get her to recovery."

Ella was floating on a cloud as she wheeled Wendy to the surgical ICU for observation and recovery. Wendy would live a long life. She had the chance to begin her life anew after her parents disowned her, free of cancer. It was everything Ella had hoped for.

She knew, of course, that what she had done would inevitably come out, but she had hoped to at least get some sleep to prepare herself for the confrontation with James.

No such luck. James was waiting at the entrance to the ICU, his arms folded and his expression thunderous.

"What the hell is this?" he hissed.

Ella took a deep breath. "I did the surgery on Wendy pro-bono."

"I can see that! What I can't understand is how

I could have made myself any clearer when I told you that you were NOT TO DO THE SURGERY!"

Ella handed Wendy's bed over to one of the ICU nurses before turning to James. "You made yourself perfectly clear, but I made an oath, James. I swore to save lives, not to save money. I chose to go against your orders. The decision is solely on me. None of the others who participated knew that the surgery was happening without your approval."

"Get out of here," James snarled.

"What?"

"Get out of my hospital and don't come back! This is one time too many, Ella! I'm not dealing with your insubordinate shit any longer. You're fired!"

Ella rocked back on her heels. She had known that she'd be in trouble, but she hadn't thought James would take it as far as firing her. "James, be reasonable. We're on the same side here. We're both out to save lives. Let's just talk about this like adults."

"The time to talk about it like adults is long past, Ella. There are no more second chances for you—or third, fourth, or fifth chances. You're a brilliant surgeon, and I hate to see you go, but I cannot have someone who is going to blow millions of dollars of hospital money without authorization. It's just not feasible."

Perhaps he was expecting her to apologize or beg, but Ella wasn't going to do either of those things. She still held that she had been in the right, and any doctor who cared about their oath would see that.

"Fine." She had to fight back tears as she turned to leave. This place had been her second home for over five years now. When you loved your work as much as Ella did, it was inevitable.

Now, she would need to find somewhere else. Ella wasn't hugely worried about finding a new job. She was one of the top surgeons in her field. Sure, she had a reputation for not playing by the rules, but was that really important when she did what she was truly supposed to do—save lives?

Ella went home and fell straight into bed, exhausted. She supposed that she didn't have to get up tomorrow, at least, being without a job.

Ella was woken what felt like minutes later, though she could tell from the sun that it must be several hours, by her phone ringing.

She answered without looking at the screen.

"Hello?" Her voice was scratchy with exhaustion and she cleared her throat.

"Hello, is the Doctor Ella Ashton?"

"Yes, that's right."

"My name is Andre Kline. I heard that you are in the market for a job."

Well, that certainly got out quickly. She hadn't even sent out any applications yet.

"Yeah, that's right."

"I'd like to offer you a position at my facility—Yarley Medical."

Ella's breath caught in her throat. Yarley Medical had one of the best surgical wards in the country. Working there would be a dream come true.

"Seriously? Yarley wants me? Do you know about my track record?"

"That's right. We heard about the surgery you did yesterday. That kind of thing may be unorthodox, but it's gained you a lot of public sympathy, and hiring you would be a huge publicity boost for the hospital, not to mention your skills as a surgeon."

"How is there already a publicity boost? I just did the surgery last night!"

"When your team heard that you were fired,

one of them did a confidential interview with a reporter. They didn't reveal their identity, but they told your story, about how hard you fought for your patient and were punished for it."

Ella's heart warmed at the thought of her team fighting for her even as she slept. She just hoped that none of them got into trouble over it.

"I'd love to accept the position."

"Excellent! Can you start on Monday?"

It was Saturday. Andre certainly moved fast.

"Let me see about getting an apartment first."

She would have to move states and finding an apartment could take weeks.

"We can fund a hotel for you while you look for an apartment."

Wow, they really did want her. Maybe being fired wasn't the disaster Ella had thought it was. This could be a new chapter in her career.

"That would be very generous, thank you."

"There is one thing I should warn you about."

Of course, there had to be one thing. This would just be too good to be true otherwise. "Alright, hit me."

"Our Head of Surgery, Dr. Valerie Bush, is not going to be at all happy about this. I'm the hospital manager and in charge of hiring, so I get the final say, but Valerie intensely dislikes rule breakers. She won't be pleased at all to have you on staff."

That could be a problem. This may be a dream job, but that dream could swiftly turn into a nightmare if Dr. Valerie Bush wanted it to be.

On the other hand, Ella had never been one to give up in the face of adversity. She was sure that this Dr. Bush could be professional—she wouldn't have become Head of Surgery if she couldn't be. Even if they didn't like each other much, the two of them could still do their jobs.

"That won't be a problem. I don't need to be friends with my boss. If she doesn't like me, well, the two of us will just have to work with that."

"Excellent! That's exactly the kind of attitude I like to see. Now, let's discuss details..."

They went over the details of the contract. The hours and the pay were more than fair. Ella would need to see the ink drying on the contract itself before she truly believed that this was all happening.

But she found herself already thinking ahead to selling her apartment and looking to buy a new one near Yarley Medical.

Thoughts of Dr. Valerie Bush were far from her

2

VALERIE

"This is such bullshit!"

"Valerie, calm down."

"Don't you tell me to calm down, Andre! How dare you stick your nose in my department?!"

"Need I remind you that I'm the hospital manager? It's my job to stick my nose in every department! Besides, have you even read her resume? She's amazing—a mercurial talent- only thirty-four and she's already pulled off some surgeries that have only been successfully completed a handful of times across the globe."

"I'm not arguing her surgical skills," Valerie admitted reluctantly. "I have looked at her resume, and she is an extremely skilled surgeon. That's not what I'm worried about. I'm worried about everything else that comes with that skill. She's not a team player, Andre. She won't fit in well here."

"On the contrary, she *is* a team player; she proved that much very recently when she convinced a bunch of doctors and nurses to go rogue with her. Working with others has never been a problem for her. What I think you meant to say is that she's not a rule follower."

"Exactly! You just said it, Andre—she convinced a group of doctors and nurses to go rogue with her! Do you even have any idea how many things are wrong with that sentence? And you HIRED this woman without asking me?"

"Honestly, Valerie, don't you think you're being a bit dramatic? This is great for the hospital. We gain an extremely talented surgeon and some great publicity for the hospital to boot."

Valerie folded her arms. "I'm not hiring her."

"It's already done. The contract was signed yesterday. She'll be here in an hour, and I expect you to be civil with her."

Valerie couldn't believe this. Running an entire surgical wing was a delicate operation, and Andre had just invited a rampaging rhinoceros into that operation. Dr. Ella Ashton was a wild card and Valerie *hated* wild cards.

Valerie stormed into her office and spent the next hour fuming quietly behind her desk, thinking about all the horrible things she wished on Andre for doing this to her. She hoped that his flash drive never went into the computer on the first try ever again, and that every vending machine he met spat his cash back out at him with as much fury as Valerie was feeling right now.

Someone knocked on her door. It was probably Dr. Ella Ashton, assuming she was even serious enough about the rules to bother to be on time to work.

Valerie took a deep breath and tried to compose herself. She wasn't happy about this, but she was going to do her best to act like an adult. Maybe this Dr. Ashton had decided to turn over a new leaf when she came here. Perhaps everything would be fine.

"Come in."

The door opened. "Hi. I'm Dr. Ella Ashton. You must be Dr. Bush?"

Valerie gaped at Ella. She had been through Ella's resume, but that hadn't had any pictures. Did

Ella have to be so stupidly attractive? Valerie's jaw was just about hitting the floor.

Dr. Ella Ashton's hair was brown and streaked beautifully with honey blonde. It cascaded over her shoulders in waves. Her bright eyes were somewhere between green and blue; Valerie couldn't tell which. Her skin was smooth and brown and Valerie wondered where her dazzling looks had been created. Valerie had never seen anyone that looked like Dr. Ella Ashton. She had a lovely hourglass figure with a slim waist, wide hips and generous breasts.

Fuck.

Valerie knew she had to say something. She was gaping at this new surgeon like an idiot. Dr. Ashton was looking expectantly at her, and Valerie did her best to pull herself together.

"Welcome, Dr. Ashton," she said stiffly. "You'll be working under Doctor Roth, our head of neurosurgery. His office is down the hall, first door to the left. He'll tell you where you need to go."

"Oh, alright then. Is there anything I should know about this place?" Dr. Ashton smiled and her smile was dazzling. Valerie took a deep breath and tried to compose herself. "You know, inside information and such."

Dr. Ashton's smile was both cheeky and charming—not a good combination for Valerie, given that it made her even more attractive than she already was.

Ugh, I hate her and I don't want her here. So why do I find her so goddamn sexy?

Valerie was irrationally angry. It was bad enough that Dr. Ella Ashton was barging into her surgical department uninvited, but did she have to look so stunning doing it?

Valerie couldn't deny that she wanted her. If she'd met Ella at a bar, the two of them would already be on their way back to Valerie's place, where she would take *everything* she wanted from Ella's body.

Dr. Ella Ashton was *entirely* Valerie's type, in a sexual way at least.

She felt her eyes roving over Dr. Ashton's breasts and hips, a pencil skirt and loose blouse doing everything to accentuate them.

Stop it, Valerie. Don't even go there.

Valerie felt her face going red and quickly forced herself to focus on Dr. Ashton's question. "Things are pretty straightforward here. Just follow the rules, and you'll be fine."

"Sure thing, Dr. Bush."

Valerie ground her teeth as Dr. Ashton turned and left.

She felt her eyes following Dr. Ashton's shapely ass and she couldn't fight the image from her head of Dr. Ashton bent over her desk. That round ass was begging for attention.

Stop it, Valerie.

She had no idea if Dr. Ella Ashton intended to follow the rules, but the very fact that she made Valerie long to break all the rules was already getting under Valerie's skin.

Valerie had long ago banned relationships—whether sexual or romantic—between employees in her department, and relationships between bosses and underlings even more so. There was absolutely no way she could sleep with this woman. It was against the rules she herself had set.

But dear God, did she want to. She cursed the fact that this woman was working here now and not just some beautiful stranger who Valerie could seduce into bed.

The rules were there for a reason, though. Valerie of all people knew that.

She closed her eyes as the memory washed over her.

. . .

Poppy was screaming. She writhed on the bed, screaming and screaming, and she wouldn't stop.

"Please! Doctor, it hurts! Fuck, it hurts so bad! Doctor Bush help me, PLEASE!"

Valerie couldn't stand it. This wasn't why she had gotten into medicine. She had wanted to heal people, not watch them in unendurable pain.

She gripped Poppy's hand. "Poppy, I swear, the pain will get less. You just need to wait it out. Your infection is severe, but the antibiotics haven't had a chance to work yet—"

Her words of attempted comfort were drowned out by another scream. Poppy's entire body was shaking and covered in sweat, but it was her face that drove Valerie crazy. The raw suffering laid bare there... it ripped at Valerie's heart.

Valerie pulled her hand from Poppy's and stumbled out of the room. "Doctor Hodson! Please, Poppy needs more painkillers."

Dr. Hodson put a sympathetic hand on Valerie's shoulder. "I'm sorry, but she's maxed out on morphine, Valerie. There's nothing more we can do until she's due for her next dose."

"But that's only in half an hour, and she's in so much pain right now..."

"I'm sorry, Valerie, but those are the rules. We can't do anything more for her."

Another gut-wrenching scream tore through Valerie's very soul.

She couldn't bear this. It was ripping her apart. Poppy was suffering in agony, all because of a stupid rule.

Valerie wasn't going to stand for it. She may just be an intern but even she could tell that what Poppy was going through was inhumane.

So, she put her code into the cart and pulled out a vial of morphine.

"I'm here, I'm here," she mumbled, rushing into Poppy's room. "You'll feel better soon, I promise."

Poppy didn't even seem to hear her, she was so wrapped up in her own pain. Valerie injected the morphine into the IV.

Almost at once, Poppy's knotted limbs started going lax. Valerie let out what felt like her first full breath since she had entered the ward this morning. This was what Poppy needed—not some stupid rule that left her in excruciating pain.

That's when it all went wrong.

Poppy's heartrate monitor started slowing and flashing red. Valerie watched in horror as Poppy's heart got slower and slower.

No, no, no, this wasn't supposed to be happening. She'd only given her the pain meds half an hour early! Surely, that couldn't affect her heart? It had to be something else...

Dr. Hodson rushed in, no doubt in response to the distressed sound of Poppy's heart monitor. Poppy's eyes rolled back in her head as Dr. Hodson checked her vitals. He grabbed her IV and spun around to face Valerie.

"What did you do!"

"I... I..."

"How much morphine did you give her?"

"I gave her the usual dose, I swear!"

"You imbecile! The usual dose given too early is enough to stop her heart! Get out of my way!"

Poppy's heartbeat flatlined, and the sound of the monitor's single long beep sent a shard of terror through Valerie's heart.

Valerie was pushed aside as Dr. Hodson grabbed the paddles and tried to restart Poppy's heart.

He tried for nearly twenty minutes, but no matter what he did, Poppy's heart wouldn't start.

Finally, Dr. Hodson put down the paddles. "Time of death, eleven-twenty-two. Congratulations, Valerie. You've just killed your patient. Hopefully in the future, you will realize that the rules are there for a reason.

. . .

Valerie had come very close to either being banned from medicine or quitting medicine after that big mistake many years ago when she was an intern. The guilt had eaten her alive, but in the end, she had decided to push through. She had changed departments, switching to surgery, and resolved to start anew and never break a rule again. She wasn't going to be needlessly responsible for any more deaths.

Valerie resisted the urge to go about her day as usual. She was too angry and unsettled to be performing surgeries right now. So, she skulked in her office and did paperwork.

The fact that Dr. Ella Ashton was already messing with her routine made Valerie so mad she wanted to scream. She tried to reason with herself. Dr. Ashton hadn't done anything wrong—yet—and she couldn't help it that she was the most stunning woman Valerie had ever seen.

Valerie knew that she couldn't allow this to throw her forever. Sooner or later, she would need to get back to her normal work routine.

For now, though, she couldn't, so she was left in her office, cursing Ella's presence here.

3

ELLA

So far, her dream job was turning out to be everything Ella had hoped for. The meeting with Dr. Valerie Bush had been a bit awkward. Valerie was clearly not pleased to have her here, but she had at least remained civil. Ella was sure that she could win her over.

Of course, things would be complicated by Valerie's appearance. Ella had spent plenty of time brainstorming how to win over her new boss. She hadn't counted on the possibility of being so attracted to her that just being in her presence left her painfully aroused.

Valerie was exactly Ella's type. Her dark blonde hair was just graying at the edges and matched her deep brown eyes perfectly. Her figure was lean and looked ready for anything; Ella was sure Valerie worked out when she wasn't doing surgeries. She must be late 50s and Ella had always had a thing for confident older women.

Ella forced herself to think of anything other than Valerie, willing her libido to go down. She couldn't go through her entire first day of work fantasizing about fucking her boss. That wouldn't do at all.

Dr. Roth seemed very different from Ella's first impression of Valerie. While Valerie had a clear no-nonsense attitude, Dr. Roth appeared to be more flexible, which was important, as far as Ella was concerned.

"You'll assist me on a tumor removal this morning, and assuming all goes well, I'll start assigning you your own surgeries."

Ella didn't need babysitting, but she understood that no one knew her or her skills here, so she didn't protest. "That sounds great. I'm looking forward to working with you."

She'd done her research. Dr. Roth was known his creativity when it came to surgeries. He had saved a number of patients who may never have made it off the table if not for his quick thinking.

"Have you looked at the clinic hours yet?"

"The clinic hours?"

"Did Valerie not tell you about the clinic?"

"No. She didn't really tell me anything; she just handed me over to you."

"That's odd. She usually gives new employees the basic rundown. I guess she was just busy. I can do it easily enough. We run a free clinic on weekends, for patients without insurance. We're always looking for volunteers to help out, if that's something you'd be interested in."

"Yeah, absolutely! I was constantly on James to set up something like that for us, but he insisted that we couldn't afford it."

"It is rather expensive to set up, but once the setup is done, we rely on volunteers and donations from medical suppliers, so it doesn't cost the hospital too much to maintain."

"That sounds awesome. I'd love to volunteer."

Ella wondered if Valerie volunteered and if they would bump into each other. She couldn't seem to get Valerie off her mind, no matter how firmly she told herself to focus on the here and now.

"Right, then if you're ready, we can go into surgery."

"Yes, I'm ready."

The tumor removal went smoothly, and Dr. Roth seemed happy with Ella's work. He handed her over to the nurse who helped manage the surgical board. Within an hour, Ella's schedule was fully booked for the day. It was going to be a busy day, but she loved that she got to dive right in.

The day flew by, and before she knew it, she was in the locker room getting changed out of her scrubs.

She was just pulling her scrub shirt over her head when Valerie walked in. Ella was sure that Valerie saw her, but Valerie didn't acknowledge her. She marched straight to her locker and grabbed her bag.

Ella couldn't help watching out of the corner of her eye.

She knew she shouldn't be watching, but this was a public locker room, after all. People got dressed here and saw each other half-naked all the time. Surely, it wouldn't be so bad if she caught a glimpse of Valerie's body with slightly less clothes, right?

Ella realized that she was frozen awkwardly with her top half on and half off. She quickly finished pulling it off and put on her own blouse as fast as possible. She could feel herself blushing, wondering if Valerie was watching.

What did Valerie think of her body? Ella snuck another glance at Valerie, but her back was turned. She didn't seem to be changing. She was simply fiddling with stuff in her bag. After a minute, Valerie shouldered her bag and headed out, still in her scrubs.

"Bye, Dr. Bush."

Valerie paused, her back to Ella and her shoulders tense. "Goodbye, Dr. Ashton," she said without turning around. Then she walked away without another word.

Ella frowned. She didn't have to be so rude. Sure, she may not be happy about having Ella here, but Valerie could at least look at her.

Well, Ella wasn't going to let that put her off. In all other ways, it had been a fantastic day. Valerie could keep her attitude. Ella didn't care. She would simply ignore it.

The rest of the week passed in much the same manner. Whenever Valerie and Ella were in the same room together, Valerie left quickly without saying much. Ella didn't know how long it would take Valerie to get the stick out of her ass, but she was quickly getting tired of this attitude.

However, for the most part, she was having too much fun to worry about Valerie. Working under Dr. Roth was great. The rest of the staff were all very welcoming, which mostly made up for Valerie's coldness.

The weekend came, and Ella signed up to work in the clinic on Saturday morning. She was both relieved and disappointed to arrive and find no sign of Valerie.

On the one hand, Ella would have liked the forced time together to hash out her differences with Valerie. On the other, perhaps it was better to have her first time in the clinic free of potential conflict and drama.

Dr. Roth was also working, and he took Valerie through the charting system they used.

"Why do you do it this way? You'd see a lot more patients if you used a shorthand system, like we do in the hospital."

"Patients in the hospital have already filled out extensive health questionnaires and been evaluated by interns or doctors from other departments. These patients have just walked in. We know nothing about them, so we need to be cautious in our approach and gather as much information as possible."

Ella supposed that made sense, but she still thought it would be a very slow system.

As the morning went on, she realized that her initial impression had been wrong. It wasn't just a slow system. It was a glacial system. By lunch time, she had only seen three patients. There were over thirty in the waiting room.

She took Dr. Roth aside. "Look, I know I'm new here, but you have to realize that this charting system is no good. I mean, look at this! You can't possibly need all this information about new patients. She's here for stitches in her arm. Why does the cancer history in her family matter?"

"You never know what might turn up. I know that for individual patients, some of the fields may seem unnecessary, but when you look at the information overall, it saves lives."

"How many lives are being lost because the people in the waiting room can't wait any longer? Do you realize that at least ten people have left the waiting room since this place opened because they couldn't afford to spend any more time here? People need to get to work, or care for children, or do any number of other things. We need to get a more streamlined system."

"I'm sorry, Ella, but these are the rules, and Valerie doesn't take well to rule breakers."

"I'll talk to Valerie, then. Surely, the rules can be changed."

Dr. Roth snorted. "You're welcome to try, but I highly doubt you'll make any progress trying to paddle up that creek."

"I'll talk to her," Ella repeated. "She wants to help people, just like us. Surely, she can be reasonable."

Ella knocked on Valerie's door first thing on Monday morning.

"Come in. Oh, it's you."

Ella ignored the suddenly sour expression on Valerie's face and focused on what she was here to do.

"I'd like to talk to you about the clinic."

"Oh yes, I heard you had your first shift on Saturday." Valerie looked slightly more cheerful now. "It's good of you to volunteer, especially so early on in your new job."

"Yes, well, I think it's a great clinic, but the patient intake... well, frankly, it sucks. I'm not sure if you realize how many people simply leave before they can get any care. Look at this."

Ella pulled out a list of names and reasons. "I

asked one of the nurses to chat with anyone leaving before being seen. As you can see, most of them only had a finite amount of time to spend in the clinic before they had to get back to work, or care for children, etc. Some had even come the day before as well and not been seen then either."

Valerie sighed. "I know we have more patients than we can see. It's a huge problem, but the clinic is only so big, and we don't have the funds to make it bigger, nor the resources to run a bigger clinic."

"I'm not suggesting either of those things. I think we should make changes to the patient intake protocol. The interviews for each patient take at least ten minutes when they could take under one. We only really need to know what they are in for and whether they have any medication allergies. If we skip all the other stuff, we can see triple the number of patients that we do now."

Ella knew before she even finished speaking that this wasn't going well. Valerie's eyes were practically bugging out of her head. "That's a terrible idea! We need to have a thorough patient history if we're to treat them. Those are the rules."

"So change the rules," Ella said through gritted teeth. She had no patience for blind adherence to the rules when they got in the way of patient care.

Valerie folded her arms. "I am not changing the rules. The rules are there to save people's lives. What if we were to do a procedure on someone whose history contradicted it? We could kill them!"

"If we're doing a specific procedure that has the potential for that, then we can ask the relevant questions. There's no need to ask all of those questions upfront before we know whether or not they're necessary."

"It's better to be comprehensive than sorry later."

"It's better to see the patients who actually need help! You're worried about potentially harming a patient, but what about the patients who are *definitely* being harmed because they're leaving without help?"

"You have my answer, Ella."

Ella was doing her best not to lose her temper, but it was difficult. "You're being completely unreasonable! Did you not hear anything I just said? Give me one good reason why my system wouldn't work."

"How about this? If a patient goes into crisis, the doctors aren't going to be focusing on asking the right question; they're going to need to do the procedure that saves them as soon as possible. We need to have that information upfront, so that it's there if we need it."

Valerie had a point there, but her point still didn't outweigh the lives that could be saved if they did things Ella's way. "So you talk to the doctors. Send them on a training course if need be. Show them how to handle the stress of a crisis and how to ensure they maintain control of themselves well enough to remember to ask the right questions."

"I can't count on that. It's a nice idea, Ella, but it simply won't work. I am not changing the rules. Not for you; not for anyone."

"That's stupid! You could be helping so many more people if you'd just be a little more flexible about the rules!" Ella realized she was shouting, but she couldn't help herself.

"Do you know what happens when doctors are flexible about the rules? People die, Ella!" Valerie was shouting now, too. She stood up and came around her desk, putting them standing a few feet from each other. Ella didn't remember standing up, but she was now practically chest to chest with Valerie.

It did *not* help her to notice how sexy Valerie was when she was angry. If anything, that just made Ella even more pissed than she already was. It was bad enough that Valerie was shooting down her idea for no good reason. Did she have to look so ravishing while doing it? It wasn't fair.

"People are dying now! Do you even bother to do follow ups on the patients who leave? Do you even care, or do your rules forbid you from doing so?"

"Fuck you, Ella! Don't you dare pretend to know how I feel! You think that if I had the manpower to be doing follow ups, I wouldn't be doing so already? I'm not superhuman! I don't have access to more resources than the hospital is able to give!"

"You have the ability to change the rules, and you're refusing to do so—to the detriment of your patients!"

"ENOUGH! I won't hear any more of this. Get out of my office. We can discuss this more when you decide to be reasonable."

"Well, that'll make one of us," Ella snarled. She resisted the urge to kick the desk on her way out. She wasn't able to stop herself slamming the door like a teenager and couldn't help the small wave of satisfaction it gave her.

She stormed through the hospital, sending

doctors and nurses scurrying away at the sight of her. She must truly look ominous, and Ella made an effort to calm herself.

She wasn't going to let the argument with Valerie ruin her whole day. She had made her case, and Valerie had shot her down. Those lives that were lost because of the stupid intake system were on Valerie's head, not Ella's. There was nothing more Ella could do. She should just leave it there.

Only, she *couldn't* leave it there. She didn't have it in her, not when she could be saving more lives by doing it her way.

She'd have to figure out a way to do this. Valerie would find out eventually, but if Ella had positive results to show her, she would have to come around. In the end, doctors were scientists, and most would relent when presented with solid data.

So, she looked up Valerie's schedule and found a time where she was booked up for a solid week. That's when Ella would make her move. She applied for a few days of leave so that she could spend that week in the clinic. One way or another, she would show Valerie that her way would work.

"Good news! We have a new intake system."

Ella breezed in with the printouts she had made the previous day and started handing them out to the nurses and doctors working in the clinic.

"You got Valerie to approve this?" Stephanie asked doubtfully.

"Valerie can be reasonable," Ella said cryptically. She wasn't lying. She was sure that Valerie *could* be reasonable, even if Ella hadn't seen evidence of it yet. Hopefully, that evidence would come when Valerie saw how much better the new system was working.

"Well, this will certainly make things easier on us nurses as well as the doctors." Stephanie ran her hand down the list of changes. "We'll need to be careful to remember to ask the relevant questions when doing procedures, but as long as we do that, this should save time and lives."

"Exactly. Now, let's get to work."

Even Ella was a bit surprised at how well her new system worked. By lunchtime, they had almost gotten through the entire waiting room. When evening came, there were only two patients who had yet to be seen.

"Don't worry, I'll lock up," she told Dr. Johnson, a resident in the psychiatry department who also volunteered regularly and was in charge of locking up for the night. "I just want to see these two patients."

"I'll stay a little later, too, and we can each see one. I can't believe we got through everyone. I don't think that's ever happened before."

Everyone had been invigorated and inspired by how well the new system worked. It showed in their work, too. People were more efficient when they felt empowered, like they were swimming rather than drowning.

Ella saw her last patient and waved to Dr. Johnson as she left. This was brilliant. Surely, when Valerie looked at the numbers, she would agree.

4

VALERIE

After a solid week with no days off, Valerie was looking forward to her weekend. She would take Saturday morning off to go to the gym and spend the afternoon working in the clinic. Saturday afternoons were always manic, and they could use all the volunteers they could get.

When she arrived in the clinic, Valerie was surprised to see the waiting room much emptier than usual. She was halfway through seeing her first patient when she realized that the doctors to either side of her had already seen three patients in the time she had seen one. How were they doing it? They had better not be slacking or cutting corners; that's how people died.

After she was done with her patient, Valerie didn't take on a new one just yet. She paused to watch, and she was horrified by what she saw.

"Doctor Johnson! What are you doing?"

"Um... I don't understand. What do you mean, Doctor Bush?"

"May I speak to you in private?"

Valerie drew Dr. Johnson away from her patient and out of earshot. "You just skipped the entire patient questionnaire and went straight to treating him!"

"What are you talking about? I did everything on the questionnaire."

Doctor Johnson showed Valerie a small slip of paper, which had just four questions on it, rather than the list of over thirty that it was supposed to be.

"What is that? Where's the proper, full-length questionnaire?"

"We dispensed with it in favor of the new system. I—wait, did you not approve this?"

Things started to click together in Valerie's head. "Who gave you this new questionnaire?"

"It was Doctor Ashton."

"I knew it," Valerie hissed.

"I'm so sorry. I didn't realize you hadn't approved it. I thought Ella said you did, though now I'm thinking back to it, I never actually heard her say that. I guess we all just assumed that she had your permission for the change."

Valerie resisted the urge to snap at Dr. Johnson when it really wasn't her fault. This was all on Ella.

"Bring back the old protocols at once. I never authorized this ... this disaster waiting to happen."

"But, Doctor Bush, it's working."

"What?" Valerie snapped.

"Look at the waiting room. Have you ever seen it this empty? We've seen all the patients who came in every day this week, and we haven't had a single bad outcome because of the new system."

Valerie wanted to dismiss Dr. Johnson's argument out of hand, but she couldn't deny that the waiting room did indeed seem emptier than usual.

"Show me the numbers of patients in and out, as well as their charts. I want to see everything."

If a mistake had been made, Valerie would find it, and then she would have Ella. If Ella had compromised patient care, Valerie could get her fired for this.

She didn't see any more patients that day but

spent the entire afternoon locked up in the small clinic office, going through files.

The more files she went through, the more aggravated she became.

No matter how hard she looked, Valerie couldn't find a single mistake. It seemed that so far, Ella had been absolutely right. They were finally getting through the patient volume they needed to in order to see everyone, and no one had been hurt.

Indignation and anger welled up within Valerie's chest, making her wish she was back at the gym so that she could beat up the boxing bag until she felt better. How dare Ella do this without her permission?! How dare she succeed?!

Of course, Valerie was glad that they were helping more patients without compromising care, but she was still angry that Ella had gone behind her back to do it.

The real question was, what should Valerie do now? She couldn't in good conscience walk back the changes Ella had made, no matter how much she wanted to. Those changes were saving lives, just like Ella had said they would.

Valerie ground her teeth as she glared down at

the numbers. No, she couldn't keep everyone to the old intake system in light of these numbers.

However, she also couldn't give Ella the idea that it was okay to go around breaking the rules. Ella had been lucky this time, but sooner or later, if she kept breaking rules, someone was going to get hurt—maybe even killed.

Valerie had to get Ella under control. A swift punishment would surely teach her a lesson.

"I'm *what?*"

"You heard me, Ella. You're suspended for a week, without pay. What you pulled was reckless and dangerous, and I won't have that kind of behavior among my staff."

"Oh yeah? Because I was in the clinic yesterday and they were still using the new intake system. Why is that I wonder?"

Valerie was once more taken by the desire to hit something. She settled for clenching her hands into fists. "I've told them to keep the new system, but that's beside the point—"

"No, that's exactly the point. I was right and you know it. If you didn't, you wouldn't have hesitated to change the system back. So you're punishing me for knowing better than you?"

"I'm punishing you for breaking the rules," Valerie gritted out. "No matter how this turned out, you would have been punished. You're just lucky your little experiment worked out. Had it not, you would not be suspended; you would be fired. As it is, you're skating on thin ice. If you want to stay here, you're going to have to learn to follow the rules. I don't tolerate rule-breakers in my staff, and that includes you."

Ella glared right back at her. "You just don't want to admit you were wrong. Grow up, Valerie! You're an adult. Sometimes, you're wrong, and it won't kill you to admit it."

"You *will* behave, Ella, one way or another." Either Ella would fall in line, or she would be out of the line altogether. Valerie wouldn't hesitate to fire her if necessary.

Ella stepped in closer and tilted her chin up to look at Valerie. "Make me," she challenged.

And oh, how Valerie longed to kiss her. She wanted to plunder Ella's mouth and make her obey through her actions if she couldn't do so through her words.

She imagined fucking Ella hard against the

desk, denying her release until Ella begged to be allowed to follow the rules.

The image was so arousing that it was almost painful to resist, but Valerie forced herself to take a step back.

It was against the rules—her rules she herself had made. She hadn't made herself popular when she had banned relationships between employees, but she was convinced it was the right thing to do. That kind of fraternization just made things so complicated, and they couldn't afford to have those kinds of complications getting in the way of patient care.

"I can't make you do anything, Ella." Valerie hated that she was slightly out of breath, even though she hadn't been moving. "I *can* tell you that your behavior will not be tolerated. Any rule breaking is not taken lightly, as you now know. Whether you want to work for Yarley Medical is up to you. Just know that if you keep going like you are now, you won't be working here for much longer. Now please get out of my office."

Before I break and start ravishing you.

Valerie didn't miss how Ella's eyes flicked to her lips and wondered if Ella was going to kiss her. Valerie didn't know whether to hope for it or not.

On the one hand, she desperately wanted Ella, but on the other, if Ella kissed her, Valerie wasn't sure if she'd have the strength to push her away.

Eventually, Ella shot her one last glare and spun on her heel, striding out of the office.

Well, Valerie had at least bought herself an Ella-free week. She could use this time to re-center and try to forget about the lustful thoughts she had about her young employee. Aside from the boss/employee issue, Ella had to be twenty years younger than her.

It is too much of an age gap, Valerie. Even if she does keep challenging you with those big innocent aquamarine eyes.

Unfortunately, while Ella was suspended from work, Valerie hadn't thought to suspend her from the clinic. Even if she had thought of it, she probably wouldn't have done it. Turning volunteers away from the clinic would just be stupid.

In the surgical wing, there were other surgeons who could cover Ella's shifts, and there was always the option to call her in should there be a case too advanced for the on-call neurosurgeons. In the clinic, if they were a doctor down, they saw fewer patients, which meant more people went home without being seen.

That's why, the very next day, Valerie found herself working side-by-side with Ella in the clinic. When she saw Ella, Valerie seriously considered turning around and going home, but she decided that she wasn't going to let Ella chase her away from work she found fulfilling. If there was a problem between them, Ella could leave.

To Valerie's indignation, Ella seemed perfectly calm in her presence. Either she was more forgiving than Valerie, or she was the world's best actress.

Ella's lovely long hair was loose and framing her face. Valerie couldn't stop imagining tangling it in her fingers.

Valerie grudgingly admitted to herself that in this case, she could do with taking a leaf out of Ella's book. For now, the two of them still had to work together, and that meant they needed to figure out how to have at least a passable working relationship if they were to help their patients.

Valerie managed to get through the day without interacting with Ella much, but she did watch her.

A lot of surgeons, especially the ones who were really good at what they did, were brilliant at surgery but terrible at patient interactions. Ella wasn't like that. She was a kind, calming presence to all of her patients, and they seemed at ease in her presence.

Valerie had to work hard not to let her bad mood ruin things for her patients. She did her best to focus on helping the people in front of her and not think about how pretty Ella looked when she was comforting a sick child or reassuring worried family members.

She thought once more about the moment when she had nearly kissed Ella.

Valerie hadn't kissed anyone in years. It wasn't that she didn't have sexual urges, but she had made the decision a long time ago not to act on them.

Her job was her life. She didn't want anything to interfere with that. Every relationship she had ever tried had eventually fallen apart because the woman in question didn't understand her commitment to her career.

Most people expected you to prioritize them above your work. When your work saved lives, it wasn't that simple.

Even after she had given up on relationships, Valerie had tried to have purely sexual relationships. She was only human, after all, and she had never wanted to remain celibate forever.

However, those hadn't worked either. When you had sex, emotions tended to get involved, whether you wanted them to or not—at least in Valerie's case. She'd had her heart broken too many times by now to ever want to be intimate with anyone again.

She had an extensive drawer of toys and she made do with that. Anything else—anything with people—was simply too complicated.

Valerie finished her day in the clinic and returned home, her mind still on Ella. Watching Ella work today had been an uncomfortable experience. It would be easier if she was an awful doctor. Then Valerie could resent her in peace.

However, that wasn't the case. Ella seemed to be an amazing doctor who really cared about her patients. She was creative, though it was unfortunate that her creativity often resulted in rule breaking. Her clever mind did tend to come up with unusual solutions, though.

Just this afternoon, Valerie had watched Ella talk a young man down from a panic attack by having him describe to her everything he knew about steam engines. Apparently, she had seen him before and knew that steam engines were a special interest of his.

It had worked, and he had left calmly with a smile. Valerie had read through his chart just to check that everything was done by the book, but she hadn't been able to find any errors.

Valerie tried to read, or watch TV, or really do anything that wasn't think about Ella, but she was failing miserably. She had never met someone who was so infuriating and alluring both at once.

Valerie eventually decided to go to bed early. She would avoid the clinic for a few days and get an Ella-free week while Ella was suspended. Maybe that would get her head straight.

5
ELLA

Ella couldn't stop thinking about the almost-kiss. She was sure it was an almost-kiss. Valerie had looked seconds away from kissing Ella, but something had stopped her—the same thing that prevented her from breaking even the smallest of rules.

Valerie's brown eyes had flooded with lust instead of anger, just for a second. Ella was sure of it.

Ella wondered what had happened to Valerie. That kind of rigidity didn't come out of nowhere. Something had made Valerie the way she was, and Ella felt sure that if she could just figure out the source, she could help Valerie work through her issues.

Of course, Valerie may not want to work through her issues, and Ella was no therapist. Maybe she should leave that kind of thing to the professionals. Sticking her nose in her boss' business was probably a bad idea.

Kissing her boss was probably a bad idea too, but that didn't stop Ella from dreaming about the possibility.

Valerie was just so sexy, especially when she was all fired up and asserting her authority. Ella knew that, ultimately, they were on the same side. They were both passionate about helping their patients. It was just too bad that their passions clashed in the logistical department.

Ella spent most of her suspension working in the clinic. They always needed more hands there, and it was kind of relaxing to do work that wasn't surgery. When someone's fine motor functions didn't depend on her fingers not twitching at the wrong moment, it made for a more relaxed day.

She noticed that Valerie didn't come to the clinic again after that first shared shift. Ella wondered if Valerie was avoiding her, though of course, that could just be her being paranoid. It was entirely possible Valerie's schedule was simply full.

The week of suspension passed quickly, and before she knew it, Ella was back at work.

She didn't see Valerie much on Monday morning, but in the afternoon, she was pulled into a surgery with Valerie. The person in question had fallen off a ladder. One of the spokes had entered his chest, and he had banged his head badly enough on a rock to cause bleeding in his brain.

"I need to shock his heart."

"Not now! If his body jolts now, it's going to pull my scalpel right through his frontal cortex."

"Then hurry up," Valerie growled. "If his heart stays stopped for much longer, he won't have any brain function left for you to preserve."

"So put him on bypass."

"If I put him on bypass in this weakened state, he may never come off!"

Ella knew that she couldn't afford to argue with Valerie right now, so she put all of her focus into getting the most critical bleeding under control as quickly as possible.

"Ella..."

"There! Shock him quickly. The worst of the

bleeding is stopped. He's still oozing, but that can wait a bit, until his heart has started again."

Valerie didn't waste any time. She shocked the patient three times before his heart started, and when it did, the beat was weak and hesitant, but Valerie was on the case. Ella concentrated on what she had to do.

It was difficult to concentrate with Valerie *right there* looking like a fucking sex goddess with a scalpel. Ella's eyes were constantly drawn to Valerie's hands. She had never thought of hands as particularly sexy before, but just the sight of Valerie performing the delicate movements necessary to save their patient's heart was such a turn-on that Ella had to take deep breaths and remind herself that her patient was relying on her to be cool and collected, not unendurably horny.

Unendurably horny could wait. For now, she needed to focus on the surgery.

It would be easier to do so if she didn't notice the way Valerie kept looking at her. Unless Ella was seriously misreading her, Valerie was every bit as interested as Ella was. Her eyes were slightly darkened and her chest was rising and falling a little faster than was usual. That could be explained away by adrenaline, but Ella didn't think so.

Every time Valerie looked at Ella, she was looking at her as though she was starving and Ella was a big, juicy burger. It made Ella want to put down the scalpel and pounce on Valerie, kissing her like she'd never kissed anyone before.

For what felt like the hundredth time, Ella forced herself to look away from Valerie. She had to focus on her patient, who was relying on her.

Unfortunately, the most difficult part of the surgery was done. It was easier to concentrate exclusively on her patient when they were bleeding to death before her eyes. Less so when what was left was a few simple stitches here and there, things that even an intern could do.

For that matter, maybe an intern *should* do it. This was a teaching hospital, after all.

Ella let her eyes rove over the three interns watching avidly.

"Becky. Come here. Let me see your sutures."

Becky's eyes practically bugged out of her head as she stepped forward. She looked ready to explode with excitement, but when she took the scalpel, her hand was perfectly steady.

"Ella, are you sure that's a good idea?"

"It'll be fine, Valerie. I've seen Becky's work, and this part is a simple fix. I'll step in if anything goes wrong."

Ella gave Becky a stern look, hoping to convey her thoughts without words—that Becky had better not do anything to prove Ella wrong about her. She didn't want to look like a fool in front of Valerie, not to mention not wanting her patient's brain to suffer any more trauma than it already had.

She watched like a hawk over Becky's shoulder as Becky did the repair. It wasn't perfect, but it was pretty good for an intern.

"Great job, Becky. You need to work on your speed; if a patient is bleeding out, you're not going to have time to go that slowly. But you are still learning, and for now, going slow is much better than making a mistake. You did really well."

"Thank you, Doctor Ashton."

Becky retreated and started whispering excitedly with the other interns. Ella gave Valerie a self-satisfied smile, and Valerie rolled her eyes. She couldn't reprimand Ella, because Ella hadn't done anything against her precious rules. This was a teaching hospital, after all, and the interns all needed to start somewhere.

"Right, I think we're almost—fuck!"

Everyone knew what Valerie was swearing about. The patient's heart monitor had suddenly gone wild. Valerie frantically started checking the heart, looking for the bleed.

"Fuck, fuck, fuck—Ella, get over here! I need your hands."

Ella didn't hesitate. She handed her scalpel over to the most senior resident, who could easily finish closing the brain up for her and hurried over to stand opposite Valerie.

"Where do you need me?"

"There's a piece of shrapnel tearing up the carotid artery. Shit, I can't believe I missed it. We should have made time for a scan."

"If we did a scan before coming into surgery, he'd have been dead when he arrived!"

Even as they spoke, they were working. Ella was frantically stitching up the damage the shrapnel did as it moved, while Valerie was desperately trying to clamp the artery above it to stop it from causing further damage.

"Ha! Okay, you little bugger. Come to Momma."

She got it. Ella couldn't believe it as Valerie clamped the artery with one hand and made a small hole with a pair of plies with the other, pulling the shrapnel out in one swift motion.

It was so hot, it made Ella's knees weak, and she was forced to lock them to stop herself from swaying on the spot. Swaying on the spot right now would be fatal for her patient, and she was *not* going to let a patient die because she was inappropriately turned on during surgery.

Valerie started stitching the artery from the opposite direction, and she and Ella met in the middle. Their gloved fingers brushed, and it felt like a tingle of electricity went through Ella's whole body at that touch.

She looked up at Valerie and found Valerie staring at her. They gazed into each other's eyes for several long moments before one of the nurses cleared her throat.

Ella and Valerie jumped apart. Ella felt her face reddening as she went back up to the patient's head to check her resident's work. Finding no problems with it, she went to scrub out, a grin on her face.

This was why she did what she did. This was why she had worked so hard to get where she was —to save the patients that no one else could save. To feel like she was really making a difference.

Valerie came to scrub next to her. Ella half expected some criticism or the other. She was so used to fighting with Valerie that Valerie's next words took her completely by surprise.

"You did a really good job in there, Ella. He wouldn't have survived without you."

"I—thanks, Valerie. He wouldn't have survived without you either."

Valerie nodded. She dried her hands and reached forward for a strand of hair that had come out of Ella's scrub cap in all the chaos. She tucked it back behind Ella's ear. Ella watched her with bated breath, wondering what would come next.

"Get some rest, Ella. You've earned it."

Then Valerie turned and left, letting the door swing closed behind her.

Ella stared after her, flummoxed. What was that?

Such a display of tenderness was completely uncharacteristic from Valerie. Was she perhaps usually more prone to affection after intense surgeries? It could be her way of releasing stress and pent-up adrenaline. Yes, that made sense. It was the only theory that did. Unless... Could it be that Valerie was softening toward Ella?

Ella had to admit that she was tired of the

constant fighting. If she and Valerie could just get along… but Valerie was so darn rigid, she didn't see them getting along any time soon. Ella had never played well by the rules, and Valerie seemed to thrive on the rules. They were just too different… too different for anything ever to work between them.

If only Valerie was less attractive—actually, no. A few weeks ago, Ella might have thought that would solve the problem, but now, she wasn't sure. She was attracted to Valerie for more than her looks. She loved how passionate Valerie was about her patients.

She had watched Valerie interacting with various patients in the clinic. She had a calming, gentle manner about her. She could be fiery when it came to fighting for what she believed in, but she could also be soothing and comforting when the situation called for it.

If only Valerie could get over her thing about rules, Ella thought they could be good friends—maybe even more than that.

Valerie didn't seem to be getting over her thing about the rules any time soon, though. Ella would just have to deal with the situation as it was. She hadn't gotten to where she was by dealing in wishes and whims. The work of a surgeon was rooted in hard, cold reality.

She didn't see Valerie much over the next few days and wondered if Valerie was avoiding her. Of course, that was probably just Ella being paranoid and self-centered. Valerie was a busy woman, and it was only natural that their paths didn't intersect for a few days at a time.

Ella kept doing her job, and the work fulfilled her, but it felt like these days, half of her mind was always occupied by Valerie. It was stupid, letting one woman—a woman who probably wasn't even interested in her—get under her skin so much, but Ella couldn't help it.

Every time she found herself in a surgery with a patient who had complications with their heart, she waited with bated breath for Valerie to appear, but it was always a different cardio surgeon. Valerie had a busy time managing the whole surgical department and, of course, she needed to delegate surgeries to other surgeons, but Ella still couldn't suppress the feeling that Valerie was avoiding her.

Well, sooner or later, they would need to work together again. Then, maybe Ella could get a proper read on what Valerie was thinking.

Maybe she could figure out her own thoughts,

too, as those were tangled and confused when it came to Valerie.

All she knew was that she wanted Valerie, in more ways than one, and that having her in that way was absolutely not an option.

6

VALERIE

Valerie was so frustrated, she felt like hitting something. She was giving serious thought to installing a punching bag in her office and bringing her gloves to work with her. Sure, the other staff would think it was weird, but what was the point of being the boss if you couldn't get away with being a bit weird now and then?

She took a deep breath through her nose, trying to dispel the urge. She wasn't going to let Ella get under her skin like that. She didn't need a stupid bag in her office. She was a grown ass adult and she could control herself.

Valerie kicked at the desk, sending it skidding

along the floor and creating a sharp spike of pain in her big toe. Better her toe than her fingers. Her toes didn't perform life-saving surgeries.

Why did Ella have to be so damn attractive? Why did she need to look so fucking kissable when her nimble fingers were manipulating a scalpel around a patient's fragile brain tissue?

Valerie had to admit to herself that it wasn't just Ella's looks that were bothering her anymore. Operating with her had made one thing very clear to Valerie, in a way that hadn't truly penetrated when she had seen as much on paper.

Ella wasn't just a gifted surgeon. She was a miracle worker. Valerie had been in this field a long time and she had seldom seen someone as talented as Ella, much less had the privilege of operating with them. Give it a decade or so, and Ella would probably be the top in her field worldwide.

Valerie couldn't afford to lose her. As much as Ella's attitude toward the rules rankled at her, she couldn't in good conscience fire Ella when she knew what an asset to the hospital and their patients Ella was... hence the nearly overwhelming urge to hit something.

So, Valerie shut herself up in her office, delegating her surgeries to other surgeons in an attempt to avoid Ella. She knew that she couldn't avoid Ella forever, but she at least needed to get her emotions under control before facing her.

Ella hadn't done anything wrong—at least recently—and Valerie knew that if she had to face her now, she would snap and say something unwarrantedly harsh. Ella didn't deserve that. She and Valerie may disagree on many things, but Valerie had seen firsthand how Ella cared for people.

She saw it in the way Ella stubbornly fought for her patients, in the OR and out of it. She saw it in the way Ella cared for patients in the clinic, and how she constantly worked on her surgical skills, always trying to do better for the people who relied on her.

If Valerie was being honest with herself, sparing Ella some harsh comments wasn't the only reason she was avoiding her, but she didn't like to admit the other reason to herself.

However, there was no denying that the sweet temptation of Ella's lips was highly dangerous to Valerie and became more and more of a problem the more she saw of Ella.

If she and Ella somehow ended up in the same

room alone together... Well, Valerie honestly didn't know if she could control herself, and losing control would end in disaster for a number of reasons.

For one, it was breaking the rules, and breaking the rules meant people died. If she and Ella were distracted with each other, that took their focus away from their patients, which was sure to be fatal to someone sooner or later.

Equally important, Valerie was Ella's boss. Rules or not, it would be inappropriate of her to kiss an employee, let alone do all the filthy things Valerie was envisioning doing to Ella. The last thing she wanted was for Ella to feel like she needed to give sexual favors in order to keep her job.

Valerie was fairly certain that Ella felt the same attraction she did, but still. She didn't want to risk forcing herself on someone.

And even if none of that was a factor, their personalities were simply incompatible. Any kind of relationship between them—even if it was purely physical—would only end in fights and drama. Their previous interactions had shown that much.

Still, Valerie's mind kept coming back to that

moment she had tucked Ella's hair behind her ear. She knew she shouldn't have done it. She had seen Ella's confusion, as well as her desire, written plainly across her face.

They had just saved a patient who Valerie had thought was beyond saving, and Valerie's emotions had been running high. She'd felt beyond grateful to have had Ella there. Anyone else wouldn't have been as quick on the brain repair, and then they would have had to make an awful decision on whether to shock him and risk losing brain function or preserve his brain function and risk losing him entirely.

Ella had saved them from that decision by a fraction of a hair, but it was that fraction that had counted.

Valerie managed to avoid Ella for a week, but of course, she was never going to be able to stay away from her indefinitely.

Her pager started beeping frantically. Valerie glanced at it and choked on her sip of coffee, already leaping up.

It was a 911 call from the ER. A huge trauma was coming in—two buses had collided—and every surgeon was going to be needed. All thoughts of avoiding Ella were pushed to the back of her mind as Valerie focused on how best to organize her surgeons in a way that saved the maximum number of patients.

When she got to the ER, Ella was waiting there along with most of the other surgeons under Valerie's command.

"Alright, people. We've got a lot of traumas coming in, so get ready for a tough time. If you need help, call for it, and don't be afraid to use the interns and residents. We'll need all hands on deck to get through this."

Ella nodded along with the rest, tying her loose hair back into a bun. Valerie tried not to watch; the effort aided by the first of the ambulances arriving.

From that point on, everything was a blur. Valerie was frantically working reactively in the ER. It wasn't long before she was pulled into a surgery. The patient's heart was pierced by a piece of shrapnel and Valerie had to get it out quickly before the patient bled out from the inside.

Of course, it couldn't be that simple. There had been no time for a full scan, and no indications of any head trauma, but sometimes these things could be deceptive. About an hour into the surgery, alarms started going off, even though things were going about as well as could be expected from Valerie's side.

She glanced at the monitors and swore. "Someone bring the portable CT in here!"

In the time it took to get the machine into the OR, Valerie's patient had deteriorated badly, but there was nothing she could do except keep going on the heart repair until she figured what else was wrong.

She glanced up at the scan and felt her heart clench at what she saw. She'd seldom seen brain bleeds that big or fast.

"Fuck. We need Dr. Ashton in here. Stephanie, go get me Ella, now."

"I think I saw her heading into surgery in OR2. I think Dr. Roth is fr—"

"No! I need Ella. Get Dr. Roth to take over her surgery and get me Ella *now!*"

Dr. Roth was a good surgeon, but Valerie needed Ella's talented hands. She wasn't an expert on neurosurgery, but even she could see that a bleed this severe was almost certain to be fatal within minutes. If anyone had a chance of fixing this, it was Ella.

Stephanie rushed out of the room and returned two minutes later with Ella. Ella scrubbed at top speed and hurried into the room, breathing hard. She didn't so much as greet Valerie, her eyes already on her patient. Valerie was too busy with her own work to worry about pleasantries.

The patient's heart was going haywire trying to keep up with the chaos happening in his brain.

"More suction. Darrin, get over here! Put your hand here, hold this bleed while I sew it up."

Valerie glanced up to see one of the senior residents carefully placing his hand where Ella directed.

She looked back down at her work, trying to coax the heart into beating just a little longer. Soon Ella would have this under control... or none of it would matter anymore.

Time seemed to move strangely as Ella and Valerie worked in tandem on the patient's heart and brain. They exchanged only short sentences related to what they needed to do, but Valerie could still feel the tension thick and heavy between them. She had no chance to examine it now, and perhaps that was a good thing.

"This isn't working. Darrin, bring the CT here. I'm going to operate looking through its eyes."

That got Valerie's attention. "You can't do that!"

"Yes, I can. I can't see through brain tissue, Valerie, but the CT can. I'm going to watch the scanner and operate based on what I see there rather than what I see with my own eyes."

"No! It's against hospital policy."

"I don't care about stupid hospital policy," Ella said through gritted teeth. "I care about saving my patient's life."

"It's against hospital policy for a reason—it's too dangerous!"

"No, it's not. This technique has been used in a number of hospitals all over the world. Just because it hasn't become mainstream yet doesn't mean it's not valid."

"I don't care where else it has been used. Here, it's against the rules."

"Fuck the rules. Darrin, bring that machine here now."

"Don't you do it if you value your job, Darrin."

"If you value this patient's life, you'd better do as I say."

Darrin hesitated for only a moment before giving Valerie an apologetic look. "I'm sorry, Valerie, but I swore an oath." He brought the CT machine over to Ella, who removed her gaze from the patient's brain and looked at the screen as the scans started to show up live.

Valerie was practically ready to explode with rage. She was on the point of physically yanking Ella away. Only the knowledge that doing so would cause Ella's scalpel to drag through the patient's vulnerable brain tissue stopped her.

She opened her mouth to order Ella once again to cease and desist, but before she could, a blood vessel in the heart burst under the pressure of trying to account for the brain injury as well as the fragile repaired heart chamber Valerie had just fixed.

She forced herself to take a deep breath and focused on the patient's heart. She could scream at Ella later. This was exactly what she'd been afraid of when Ella had first come to work here. Not only was Ella tossing the rules aside like garbage, but she was convincing other doctors to do it with her.

Well, they would see about that. If this patient died, Valerie would have Ella's head on a platter for this. Brilliant surgeon or not, if her reckless disregard for rules resulted in a patient's death, Valerie would crucify her.

Time dragged on. Valerie became totally immersed in her work of saving the patient's heart.

By the time she looked up, her aching feet told her that she'd been standing for several hours.

She startled when she saw that Ella was closing up the patient's head.

"What are you doing?"

"I'm closing. I fixed it. His brain is fine. You're welcome."

Darrin was wheeling the CT scan away. Valerie ground her teeth, trying to bite back her furious diatribe. She managed to finish closing the patient's chest before finally losing control.

"Ella. Clean up and then come to my office."

Valerie scrubbed and stalked to her office to find Ella already waiting there for her and not even looking abashed at her behavior. Ella gave her a defiant look as she waited for Valerie to speak.

"Well? Don't you have anything to say for yourself?"

"The patient survived. My strategy worked. You're welcome."

"Fuck that, Ella! Your patient may have survived, but that was pure luck. You broke the rules, rules that were put in place to protect people. I am your *boss* and you *will* mind what I say."

"You may be my boss, but your authority doesn't supersede the oath I made, Valerie. I'm here to save lives, not to follow stupid rules. I'm not a surgery automaton you can control and force to follow orders; I'm a person with a mind of my own, and that mind has saved a number of patients that no one else could save. Or did you forget that you called for me when you knew that your patient was dying? If you have a problem with my work as a surgeon, then I'm all ears."

Valerie opened her mouth to continue shouting at Ella, and then closed it again. She dearly wanted to continue this argument, but the way Ella had put it was making it very difficult. No matter how hard she tried, Valerie couldn't find anything to criticize with Ella's actual skills as a surgeon. No, it was all the other chaos that surrounded her that drove Valerie mad.

She finally found another line of attack. "It's not just about surgical skills, Ella. You're not the only one in this department. We all need to work together here, and we can't do that unless there are some common rules for all of us to follow."

"I get that, Valerie, but your rigidity around sticking to those rules is just ridiculous. You need to learn to be more flexible."

"Don't you tell me what to do, Doctor Ashton!"

"Then don't you tell me how to take care of my patients!"

Fuck, why did Ella have to be so sexy when she was angry? It made Valerie even madder than she already was, and she was practically boiling over with rage already.

Valerie didn't know what to do. She couldn't fire Ella—they needed her, she was sure of that much—but she couldn't work like this, either.

Suspending her again was no good, either. Denying the hospital of a surgeon of Ella's talents was just shooting herself in the foot.

Some of her anger abated as an idea came to her. "From tomorrow, you are to report to HR first thing in the morning, an hour before your shift is due to start. I'm sending you on a catch-up course of all the hospital rules. One month long. Let's see if spending some time learning the rules will teach you to follow them better."

Ella's expression morphed into one of outrage. "Are you serious right now? I'm not some school child you can put in detention!"

"Then stop acting like one! You *will* go on the HR course and that's the end of it."

"Fine," Ella snapped, "but don't expect this to

change anything. You can have me memorize all the rules you like, but I will *never* put a rule above my patient's welfare."

Not for the first time, the idea of bending Ella over the desk and fucking her into submission crossed Valerie's mind. She needed to get Ella out of here before she did something crazy like act on that urge and end up with a sexual harassment suit to deal with.

"Get out of here, Ella. I don't want to hear anything else out of you until you can recite all the hospital rules word for word."

Ella glowered at Valerie for a moment before spinning on her heel and stalking out, looking unfairly sexy as she did it.

7
ELLA

Ella stomped through to the HR department with ill grace. She knew from asking around that she was the only person to be sent on this kind of punishment course. In fact, to her knowledge, such a course didn't even exist.

Valerie must have been up all night creating it, because when Ella got to HR, she was greeted with a thick booklet of questions and answers, as well as the equally thick booklet of hospital rules that she had been given when she joined the hospital.

Ella had read it, of course, but she hadn't memorized it verbatim.

"Hi, Ella, please sit down. Dr. Bush has

requested that you read through the rules booklet again and then answer these questions. They will be sent to her for evaluation and once you get them all correct, you will go back to your normal schedule without these sessions."

"Valerie said this was for a month," Ella grouched.

"It's a month minimum, but Valerie says that if it takes longer, then it takes longer."

Great. That was just great.

Ella sighed as she opened the booklet. She was fairly sure she could get through this fast, and the questions couldn't be that difficult. After all, how hard could regurgitating a bunch of rules be?

Unfortunately, it seemed that things wouldn't be that simple.

There were questions on the rules, for sure, but there were also multiple example questions. Valerie gave detailed scenarios of surgeries and required Ella to list how she would react according to the hospital rules.

Ella gnashed her teeth as she read the different questions Valerie had written. Valerie knew her too well. She had deliberately chosen situations in which she knew Ella's first instinct would be to break the rules in order to save her patient.

Ella knew the correct answers to the questions—at least, the answers Valerie wanted. She could lie and say that she would react according to the rules, but that didn't sit right with her.

So, she stubbornly wrote out what she would honestly do in each situation, giving reasons as to why the rules were obsolete in those cases. She didn't expect her reasons would sway Valerie and suspected she would have to redo this assignment multiple times, but while Valerie was stubborn, so was Ella, and she wasn't giving in on this point.

There were some scenarios in which following the rules was the only sensible thing to do, but Ella didn't do it because those were the rules; she did it because that was what was in the best interest of her patients.

Once her hour was up—she had only done a few pages of the very thick booklet—Ella went to the locker rooms to get changed, trying to quell her bad mood. If she was going to be doing this every morning for the foreseeable future, she would need to learn not to let it ruin her day. She loved her job and she wasn't going to let Valerie sour it for her.

The next day, she got to HR to find that Valerie had marked her answers, in red pen, no less.

Unsurprisingly, Ella had gotten a number of questions "wrong." Valerie had even written snarky responses as to why they were wrong.

As much as she was giving Ella extra work, she was giving herself extra work, too. Surely, she would get tired of this eventually.

Ella wished that she and Valerie could talk, truly talk, without arguing, for once. She felt sure that if they could just get past this rules thing, they had the potential to be good friends. However, every time Ella saw Valerie, Valerie resolutely ignored her, and Ella wasn't going to be the one to go running to her, not given how unreasonable Valerie was being.

"This is so stupid!" Ella sighed in frustration on the fourth day of her HR assignment. "I'm never going to give the answers Valerie wants. Why won't she just accept that?"

Penelope, the unfortunate HR representative who had been assigned to ensure Ella turned up for her morning sessions, looked at Ella from over her glasses. "Valerie isn't going to budge on this. You may as well just give her what she wants. Trust me, this is not a fight you're going to win."

"But *why?* I know she cares about her patients!

Why can't she see that this stance is compromising patient care?"

"Trauma does funny things to the brain," Penelope said cryptically.

"What do you mean?"

Penelope sighed. "I've been at this hospital a long time, you know, ever since Valerie was an intern. There was... an incident. Do you remember the first patient you killed?"

"Of course. I think all doctors do. It's still something that haunts me."

"Well, the first patient Valerie killed died because Valerie broke the rules. She did it with the best of intentions, trying to help her patient, but the patient died because of it. Valerie was young and had thought the rule unimportant, but it turned out that the rule was put in place for everyone's protection and going against it brought about the death of a patient who otherwise could have been saved."

Ella's hand paused on the page. "What happened?"

"She overdosed a patient on morphine. The patient was in excruciating pain and Valerie couldn't take it anymore. Unfortunately, the patient's heart was weaker than Valerie had realized, and she died a few minutes later."

Ella felt her insides squeeze with sympathy. As much as she hated Valerie's rigid insistence on sticking to the rules, given what she had just heard, she could understand it a little better.

Ella's stance on the rules was for a similar reason, after all. She had seen too many patients who could have been saved die just because of stupid policies.

For Valerie to have been responsible for a woman's death when she was so young because she disregarded the rules... Well, Ella could see why Valerie would make the assumption that breaking the rules killed people.

It was an assumption that wasn't always correct, but that didn't mean it wasn't understandable.

Unfortunately, that didn't help Ella much. Valerie seemed so entrenched in her ways that if nothing in her career so far had convinced her that she was wrong, Ella doubted that she would have much of a chance.

She sighed and looked at the booklet she was writing her answers in. She wasn't going to lie, but she could still write what Valerie wanted. Anything to get Valerie to let her off this stupid course.

She thought for a moment before writing *By the rules answer* as a heading, followed by what Valerie wanted to hear. She left out the part that she wouldn't be acting on the by the rules answer.

Valerie would probably figure that much out for herself, but Ella hoped that this would be an acceptable compromise. Valerie would see that she knew how to apply the rules, even if she wasn't going to be doing it when it came down to the rules or her patient.

At the end of an hour, Ella handed the booklet in to Penelope for what she fervently hoped would be the last time.

8

VALERIE

Valerie glowered at the booklet she had spent so much time writing. *By the rules answer*—as if she would fall for that. She knew very well why Ella had put that heading. The question had called for an account of how Ella would react. The "by the rules answer" was very clearly stating that the answer was what Valerie wanted to hear and not how Ella would really react.

Valerie wondered if this was the best she was going to get. As much as she wanted Ella to learn the rules, she didn't want to spur her into quitting. As she read through the answers, she was forced to admit that Ella did have a good understanding of how to work within the rules. If only she actually applied it to real situations.

She reluctantly sent an email to Penelope, telling her that Ella was to be allowed off her punishment course after the minimum set time of a month. Hopefully this whole experience would teach Ella a lesson. Somehow, Valerie doubted it, but she could hope, right?

As much as she hated that she was reduced to this, she continued to avoid Ella. This meant doing fewer surgeries and more paperwork in her office, but Valerie still didn't trust herself around Ella.

Just thinking about Ella's enticing curves and the way her slim fingers moved a scalpel delicately through brain tissue made Valerie unbearably horny.

More than once, she had been tempted to use one of the hospital on-call rooms to get herself off to thoughts of Ella. It would have made her life a lot easier when she could focus on anything but how badly she wanted to have Ella's tongue on her clit, but Valerie stubbornly refused to act on these urges.

Getting herself off at work would be entirely inappropriate, especially if she did it because a certain employee was looking so utterly irresistible, and she wouldn't do it. Valerie even refused to masturbate at home, because she knew that thoughts of Ella would creep in while she did so.

She hadn't come in weeks, which hardly helped matters. She was horny all the time, and the smallest interaction with Ella would send her pussy into overdrive. She found herself embarrassingly wet just from a simple conversation with Ella. And the one time their hands had accidentally brushed... Well, the urge to get herself off in the on-call room had never been stronger.

Valerie felt like she was a teenager again, unbearably horny and controlled by her urges, but she was an adult now and she wouldn't let her urges get the better of her, no matter how much her clit ached to be touched, almost painful on some days the longer it was neglected.

It had been years since Valerie had felt like this about anyone, and she didn't know what to do with it. Sure, she'd seen attractive women before, but the attraction had never taken hold of her mind and body the way it had with Ella.

There was a knock on her door, startling Valerie out of her internal dialogue, telling herself that she absolutely could not stick her hand into her pants and rub her clit to thoughts of Ella, even if it was just for a few moments.

"What!" she yelled.

Stephanie tentatively stuck her head in. "Sorry to bother you, Valerie, but there has been a plane crash a couple of miles out. They're asking if we can spare some doctors to go to the site and do triage."

Valerie forced herself to take a deep breath. Stephanie hadn't done anything wrong and didn't deserve to have her head bitten off just because Valerie had tied herself in knots.

"Of course. Get everyone we can muster at short notice, everyone who is willing to go to a potentially unstable situation. We'll meet in the parking lot in ten minutes."

Valerie spent the next ten minutes arranging a bus to take her team to the site. A part of her hoped that Ella would decline the invitation to help out, but she should have known better than that. Ella was first in line to get onto the bus. Of course she was.

Well, the scene was going to be chaos. Valerie shouldn't have any time or brain power to focus on Ella.

She watched Ella take a seat at the front of the

bus before walking to the very back, looking out of the window, forcing herself to ignore Ella altogether.

When they got to the scene, it was indeed chaos. Valerie dove right in, forgetting all about her frustrations as she scrambled to do the best she could for the horribly injured crash survivors.

Her attention was drawn by the shouts of one of the search-and-rescue guys.

"Ma'am, you can't go in there! It's too unstable."

Valerie wasn't at all surprised to hear Ella's reply. "I think I can hear someone in there. Maybe they need my help. I'm going in to check."

"Ma'am, we checked already. We got everyone out." The call from the firefighter fell on deaf ears.

Ella shoved her way past the search-and-rescue operative and started picking her way through the rubble, right into the belly of the collapsing plane.

Valerie growled under her breath as she broke into a run. No way was Ella getting herself killed on Valerie's watch. Valerie would drag Ella away from that plane herself if she had to.

"Ella! Ella, get back here right now! You're not to go in here! Ella, do you hear me?"

Ella, however, seemed to have gone selectively deaf, ignoring Valerie completely. Valerie kicked rubble aside as she dashed after Ella, reaching her just as she stepped into the cabin.

She grabbed Ella's shoulders, yanking her back. "Not a chance," Valerie snarled. "You're coming with me, whether you like it or not."

She knew she was stronger than Ella and would wrestle her out of here if need be.

Ella's angry response was drowned out by a thundering crash.

Ella grabbed Valerie and pulled her forward just in time to avoid the side of the cabin collapsing on her.

They landed on the ground, with Valerie's body covering Ella's. She didn't even have time to appreciate the feeling of Ella's body pressed against hers, because they were both coughing up dust and small pieces of rubble were falling all around them.

Valerie rolled off Ella, coughing until her lungs were clear.

"What the fuck did you do!" Valerie demanded as soon as she could talk. She stared hopelessly around them. The way out was completely blocked. The only light came through the cabin's windows. The metal around them was completely collapsed. It would probably take hours for search and rescue to dig them out.

Ella wasn't listening to Valerie. She was already searching the body of the small plane. It was empty.

"FUCK!" There were tears in Ella's eyes as she realised the mistake she had made and now they were trapped.

The reprimand died on Valerie's lips. She wanted to scream at Ella for putting them in this position, but in the face of Ella's distress, she couldn't bring herself to do it.

Ella had risked her life to save someone she thought was in there and there was nobody there; she was understandably upset. There would be time for reprimands—time Valerie would use to its full advantage—but this was not it.

Valerie looked at Ella, her incredible aquamarine eyes glimmered in the dim light. Her smooth brown skin and honey streaked ponytail were covered in dirt and debris from the collapse.

Valerie thought she had never looked more beautiful.

"I really thought I heard someone. Must have been from outside of the plane though."

Valerie sighed and leaned back against the

cabin wall. "Well, I don't suppose there's much to do but wait for them to dig us out."

"Nope," Ella said gloomily. "I guess you were right—at least this time."

"About what?"

"If I'd followed the rules and stayed out of here, I'd be out there right now saving patients. Instead, I'm stuck in here, and people are dying because I'm not there to help them."

Valerie dearly wanted to say, "I told you so," but Ella sounded so dejected that she decided that, too, could wait.

"Beating yourself up for past mistakes is a waste of energy. You can only learn from them and move forward."

Ella nodded. "I know."

The two were silent for a while, listening to the sounds of search and rescue trying to dig them out. It must be a difficult task, as they obviously couldn't do anything that would cause the plane to collapse any further. This might take a while.

Valerie glanced at Ella out of the corner of her eye. She was so pretty, even covered with dust, blood and tears. Even in this state, Valerie would totally kiss her if she could. She wondered what Ella's lips would taste like, and if she would get their natural flavor from underneath all the dust and salt.

She realized that she was staring at Ella's lips and forced herself to look up into Ella's eyes, only to find that Ella was staring at her lips as well.

Shit. This was not going in a direction Valerie felt like she had much control over, and she knew all too well that when she lost control, people died. Being stuck in an enclosed space with Ella for hours was the last thing she needed, but it wasn't like she was being given any choice in the matter.

"Well, we're here. We may as well talk."

"I don't want to talk," Valerie said shortly. If she got into another screaming match with Ella, one where she couldn't remove herself from the situation, she knew that fucking Ella into submission would be an all-too-real possibility.

"Valerie... we both know that we're on the same side here. If we could just get over the logistical issues driving us apart—"

"But we can't, Ella. You've made it clear that you have no respect for the rules, and that's not a stance I can respect."

Ella opened her mouth, took a deep breath, and closed it again. "I don't want to argue with you, Valerie." She was certainly showing more self-control than Valerie had at the moment, but she probably wasn't so horny that she could barely control herself.

Valerie gritted her teeth and clenched her jaw. If Ella could have the self-restraint not to get into yet another argument, then Valerie could too. No way was she going to be outdone by a rule-breaker like Ella.

They sat in silence for a little while longer, the tension between them growing. Ella kept glancing at Valerie's lips, and it was doing nothing to help Valerie's libido go down.

The cabin groaned around them as the rescue team tried to get to them, but no further chinks of light appeared. Valerie sighed and brought her knees up to her chin. The movement put pressure on her clit and she had to stop herself from groaning aloud. She glanced at Ella, noting the curve of her chest, even under the scrubs.

She was getting wet. This was *so* not the time, but her body wasn't responding to her urgent commands. Valerie's clit started throbbing as she sneaked another glance at Ella, who seemed to be breathing harder than before. Valerie had to resist the urge to press her legs together tighter. That led down a road she simply could not find herself on.

The cabin around them suddenly shifted violently, sending Ella flying into Valerie's lap, right between her legs. Valerie couldn't help it. Ella's knee was pressed right up against her aching clit and she moaned loudly, her eyes slipping shut.

"Valerie? Are you okay? Are you hurt?"

Valerie shook her head, breathing hard. Ella was shifting around, trying to get her balance on the new angle, and if she didn't remove her knee *right now* Valerie was going to come.

Valerie's eyes fluttered open as she prepared to tell Ella to move back, but then she met Ella's gaze, and the words died in her throat. Ella's eyes were darkened with lust, the same as Valerie knew hers must be.

The next thing she knew, Ella was leaning forward and capturing her lips in a kiss. The forward motion pressed her knee even harder between Valerie's legs, and Valerie couldn't help spreading her legs a little wider, allowing Ella better access.

Valerie kissed Ella as though she was drowning, and in truth, she was—drowning in overwhelming desire that had plagued her for weeks now.

Their tongues tangled together in the most

delicious dance. Ella moaned into the kiss and wriggled her knee from side to side. Ah, fuck, Valerie was going to come. She was practically devouring Ella's mouth as she spread her legs wider, breaking away from the kiss to gasp for air as her legs started to tighten—

The cabin shifted again, throwing Ella off her and sending light spilling in through the hole the search- and-rescue people had ripped in the wall of the plane.

Valerie was left lying limply against the cabin wall, her legs still spread wide, gasping for breath. She was so close, she felt like a stray breath of wind could knock her over the edge. All she needed was just one more touch to her clit and she would be coming… but a search-and-rescue guy was sticking his head into the cabin and holding out his hand toward them.

"Come on, let's get you out of here, doctors."

Valerie remained on the floor, afraid that even bringing her legs together to stand up would bring enough pressure to her clit to make her come. Her thighs were so tense they were trembling and her hands were clenched into fists. She was panting harshly, her arousal almost unbearable.

Ella glanced between Valerie and the guy.

"We're okay here, now, thanks. Why don't you go back to helping the others? We can get out ourselves. No, really, go on. We'll be right out."

He reluctantly left, and Ella knelt down by Valerie's side.

"Valerie? Do you want... help?"

Valerie knew exactly what Ella was offering. Every part of her ached for just one more touch from Ella, one more touch to send her over the edge.

Valerie shook her head jerkily. Now was not the time.

"I'm fine. You go on."

"I am not leaving you here. Come on, up you go."

The next thing she knew, Ella was hauling her up by her right arm. Valerie moaned and almost doubled over as her body threatened to come, but it wasn't enough. She staggered after Ella, who if she wasn't mistaken, also seemed a little unsteady on her feet.

They re-entered the bedlam that was the scene of the accident. Even though it had taken a little time for them to be dug out, there were still patients everywhere who needed their help.

Valerie ignored her body's frantic pleas for her

to get somewhere where she could be alone and release the unbearable tension she was feeling.

She had a job to do.

9

ELLA

"Valerie? Can we talk?"

"Why?" Valerie snapped.

Ella understood Valerie's frustration. It had been clear that Valerie had been on the brink of coming several hours ago when they were trapped in that plane, and it was obvious by the stiff way she was holding her body that she hadn't taken the time to relieve herself since then.

Ella wondered why. It was clearly affecting Valerie's temper. It must be more of Valerie's obsession about rules. While there was no set rule about getting yourself off in the bathroom, Ella supposed that it could well be implied in the "no sex in the hospital" rule.

She wondered how long Valerie had been denying herself for, to be that close that quickly. Ella loved that she had such an effect on Valerie but couldn't help feeling sorry for her in the state of obvious need she was in.

She had already taken the time have a quick orgasm in the nearest bathroom. It hadn't taken long, given how turned on she'd been from Valerie's kiss. She had discovered the hard way from working with Valerie that trying to operate while she was painfully aroused was difficult and sapped her concentration quickly. Best to take care of it before she got into the OR.

Valerie didn't seem to share this opinion. She was currently glowering at Ella, as though her self-denial was Ella's fault.

"Please? I think we're long overdue for a talk. We could have died today. I... I'd like to talk about it, if that's okay with you."

Valerie's expression softened a little. "I... okay. Let's go to the cafeteria, shall we?"

Ella followed Valerie to the cafeteria, watching her tight ass swaying enticingly from side to side as she walked.

Valerie's shoulders and hips were still as tense as a drawn bowstring. Ella couldn't help wondering what it would take to get Valerie to relax. How long would it take Valerie to come if Ella started licking her clit? Judging by the state Valerie was in, probably not long.

Her pupils were still huge when she looked at Ella. She was clearly still deeply in her aroused state, and not even surgery seemed to have dragged her out of it.

Watching Valerie like this was such a turn on for Ella that she was already considering when she could next get away to the bathroom for a little alone time.

They got something to eat and drink and sat down. There were a few seconds of loaded silence between them before Ella spoke.

"It seems really petty now, doesn't it? This rivalry we have. We could have died, and here we are, fighting each other when we're really on the same side."

Valerie sighed, her shoulders slumping slightly in defeat. "I guess so. I don't want to keep fighting with you, Ella. It's just…"

She trailed off, not needing to continue. Neither of them could seem to help themselves.

"I think we should start over. We could be good friends, Valerie, I truly believe that."

Valerie looked doubtfully at Ella. "Friends?"

"Yeah, friends. Look, we're both exhausted and filthy. How about we go home, shower and get some sleep, and then tomorrow, we can get lunch together. We can get to know each other a little better."

Despite their multiple interactions, Ella knew very little about Valerie other than she loved sticking to the rules.

"I'd like that," Valerie said softly. "A fresh start."

"Yeah, exactly. A fresh start."

Ella wanted to kiss Valerie again, but she had a feeling that it wouldn't be welcomed. Something powerful must be holding Valerie back, or she would have pounced on Ella already. Ella didn't want to force Valerie into doing something she didn't want to do.

She was sure that if she was to kiss Valerie now, one thing would lead to another and they would end up naked in one of the on-call rooms together.

She was also almost equally sure that Valerie would regret it later. Her body's reactions were running haywire right now and it would be unfair of Ella to take advantage of that.

If she was going to get Valerie into bed, she wanted it to be without regrets on either side.

Maybe, once they had forged a firmer friendship, it would be a real possibility, one that they would both get value from and look back fondly on.

It almost hurt to do, but Ella smiled at Valerie, took her food and left.

The next day, she worked her entire schedule around making sure that she had lunch at the same time Valerie did. She didn't want to miss their lunch date, even though it wasn't actually a date.

Valerie must have arranged her schedule carefully as well, because she was waiting in the cafeteria when Ella arrived.

They stood briefly in the line for food before taking a table together.

"How has your day been?" Valerie asked politely. Ella forced herself not to laugh, but it was difficult when she could probably count on one hand the number of polite things Valerie had ever said to her.

"It was pretty good. Fairly basic stuff, but necessary. The interns and residents learned a lot."

"I've seen you work with them. You're a really good teacher, Ella."

Ella glowed under the praise. "Thanks. I was worried I wouldn't be. You know, a lot of surgeons are excellent in their chosen fields but crap at teaching, and a lot of the best hospitals are teaching hospitals. I want to be good at all of my job, the teaching part included."

"Well, you are. They all love you."

"What about you? Do you enjoy the teaching part?"

"It's satisfying, in its own way, but nothing will ever compare to surgery for me. There's nothing like having a living heart in your hands, knowing that you are the only reason it's beating."

"I feel similarly. Seeing a patient walk or use fine motor functions that I know are only possible because I excised a tumor or otherwise saved their brain function... Well, it's why I do my job. It's why I love it."

"What would you be if you couldn't be a surgeon?"

The question took Ella by surprise, and she wasn't entirely sure she wanted to answer. "You'll laugh."

"I won't."

"Fine... I'd have been a lawyer."

Valerie raised an eyebrow. "A lawyer?"

"A human rights lawyer," Ella explained. "I've seen too many patients turned away from life-saving treatments just because they couldn't pay. If for some reason I couldn't be a surgeon, I probably would have tried to save lives in a different way by tackling that injustice."

"Ah, that makes sense."

"What about you? If you couldn't be surgeon?"

"I guess I've never really thought about it. Being a surgeon is all I ever wanted. I don't know who I'd be without my work."

"I can understand that. I know that I help my patients, but I sometimes feel like I'd be the one who is lost without them."

Valerie nodded. "Tell me more about yourself, Ella. We've been working together for weeks now, but I barely know anything about you. What do you do when you're not working or volunteering in the clinic?"

"Well, those two things scarcely leave time for other hobbies."

Valerie chuckled. "Don't I know the truth of that. I manage to sneak in some reading now and then, but not nearly as often as I would like."

"What kinds of things do you read?"

Valerie's cheeks got slightly pink, but she answered anyway. "I'm a sucker for romance novels, actually. Which is ironic, given that I have no interest in romance personally."

"Why not?"

Valerie hesitated. "I've tried it before, many times. I really wanted to find love, but it never worked out. My career always has been and always will be my first love. Most people don't appreciate being put second to their partner's job. Eventually, I gave up. There's only so much heartbreak one person can take."

Ella wondered if Valerie had ever tried dating another doctor who would understand the demands of the job but decided not to ask. She and Valerie were only just forming a tentative connection between them, after all, and she didn't want to push too hard and break the thin thread they were creating.

"I've dated before, but never really seriously. I guess I just haven't found someone I wanted to be serious about. I suppose if I do, I'll run into the same problems you have, but I'll just have to deal with that if it happens. I'm not willing to give up on love yet."

"I hope you find it," Valerie said softly. "You're a good person, Ella. I'm glad you weren't crushed back there. I would have hated it if anything happened to you."

Once again, Valerie had taken Ella by complete surprise. Her tender words were in such opposition to the constant fighting Ella had had to endure over the last few weeks that she was momentarily shocked into silence. Eventually, she found her voice.

"I'm glad you're okay, too, Valerie. We may disagree on many things, but I know that you fight for your patients just as fiercely as I do, and I really admire that about you."

There was a pause as they both considered the unsaid things between them—the things that would no doubt lead to a screaming match in the middle of the cafeteria.

Ella decided it was time to steer the subject into safer waters. "So, who is your favorite romance author?"

"You've never heard of her."

"Oh, really? I have read some romance, myself. Like I said, I haven't given up on love. I may not have found it yet, but that doesn't mean I can't live vicariously through fictional characters."

Valerie grinned. "Okay, then. Emily Hayes."

"I haven't read her stuff yet, but I have heard of her. I'll have to check her out!"

They spent a good ten minutes discussing Emily Hayes, Anna Stone, Jae, Margaux Fox and Radclyffe, before moving on to other shared interests. Ella was surprised to find she had a lot in common with Valerie, from hobbies to political views to funny patient stories.

She got so engrossed in talking to Valerie that she didn't even realize that her lunch was long over. She had, in fact, gone twenty minutes over time.

Valerie suddenly glanced at her watch and leaped up as though she'd been electrocuted. "We're late! We should have been back to work twenty minutes ago."

Ella looked at her watch and hastily got up as well. "I guess we got distracted."

"That's not acceptable! It's against the rules!"

Ella resisted the urge to roll her eyes with difficulty. Valerie looked like she might cry, or scream, Ella wasn't sure which. She tentatively put a hand on Valerie's shoulder. "Something tells me you haven't been late from lunch in quite a while. It's okay to make a mistake every now and then,

Valerie. I know you didn't mean to break the rules."

Valerie took several deep breaths. "Yeah. You're right. We should get back to work, though. This was nice, Ella. Do you... Do you want to do it again tomorrow?"

"Tomorrow sounds perfect. Maybe we could go to a real restaurant? I must admit, the cafeteria food leaves something to be desired."

"True enough. There's a diner down the road that does great toasted sandwiches."

"The diner it is, then."

They both went their separate ways. Ella couldn't stop smiling. She had a good feeling about this. From the beginning, she had felt like she and Valerie could be good friends if they could just get past the issues they were constantly arguing about. Now, it seemed like that was a real possibility.

She couldn't wait to see where this led.

10

VALERIE

Once again, Valerie found herself leaving lunch with a silly grin on her face. It had become a pattern over the past three weeks, meeting Ella at the diner for lunch. She made every effort to make her own lunch break happen when she knew Ella would be between surgeries. She had been surprised to find that she actually really liked Ella when they weren't fighting.

They had so far carefully steered away from topics that were bound to cause friction between them, and their working relationship was much better for it. Of course, Valerie knew it was only a matter of time before a situation came up where

Ella felt it was necessary to break the rules, but she was just trying to enjoy the peace while it lasted.

It was nice. The only problem was that, as sexy as Ella was when she was angry, she was even more irresistible when the two of them weren't banging heads. Valerie was unbearably turned on in Ella's presence, but she still stubbornly refused to masturbate to the thought of her.

Thoughts of Ella were so prominent in her mind that this meant she didn't get to masturbate at all. It left her frustrated, to say the least, but that frustration was always worth it when she sat down across from Ella at the diner and started exchanging news about their day.

The two of them walked back to the hospital together once the lunch hour was over. "What do you have up next?"

Valerie groaned. "Paperwork. It never ends in this job. How about you?"

"Surgery. A young man with a severe speech impediment. We recently found on the MRI that it's caused by a benign tumor. I'm going to remove it."

That all sounded above board to Valerie. She was relieved that yet another day seemed to be passing when she wouldn't have to argue with Ella. "Lucky you. I wish I could join you."

"Well, I'm sure a big trauma will come in sooner or later and pull us into a surgery together."

"Hoping for a huge trauma is probably not a good idea, Ella."

Ella made a face at her. "You know what I mean."

Valerie chuckled. "I do. Come on, we're going in the same direction anyway. I'll walk you to the OR."

They got into the elevator and waited for it to take them up to the third floor.

It got to the second floor and went a bit higher then stopped.

Valerie frowned and clicked the third-floor button again. The elevator shuddered slightly before going still again.

Well, fuck. When was the last time these elevators had been serviced? Valerie wasn't in charge of that, but she knew that management sometimes skimped on what they considered unessential expenses.

"Great. That's just great," Ella muttered. She pressed the help button, and a minute later, a tinny voice came through.

"Hello?"

"Yes, hi. This is Dr. Ella Ashton. I'm stuck in an elevator with Dr. Valerie Bush. It's the one on the far right of the lobby."

"Got it. We'll send a technician to get you out. You just hang tight."

So, they waited. Valerie knew that she wasn't a patient person. She checked her watch multiple times. She could be getting through her paperwork right now, but instead, she was stuck in an elevator with Ella.

She glanced at Ella and found Ella watching her. More specifically, watching her lips. Yeah, this wasn't good. How the hell was Valerie supposed to resist Ella for an unspecified amount of time in an enclosed space like this?

The tinny speaker crackled to life.

"Okay, good news, doctors. We know what the problem is. Bad news is that it'll take at least two hours to fix."

"TWO HOURS?! That's unacceptable!" Valerie spluttered.

"Sorry, Doctor Bush, but that's just the way it is. Don't worry, we'll get you out of there. Try not to panic."

Valerie wasn't panicked; she was pissed. This

was *so* unfair. Ella sighed and sank to the floor, taking out her phone. "I'd better postpone my surgery."

How could she be so calm about this? Valerie was ready to bite someone's head off, but there was no one here except Ella, who was clearly not at fault.

Valerie sighed noisily and sat down next to Ella with ill grace. "This sucks."

"Yeah, I wish I didn't have to postpone the surgery. Still, I can move around my schedule. It's not the end of the world. At least help is on the way."

Valerie admired Ella's attitude and resolved to try to be more like her. Ella was right. It wasn't the end of the world. They were both healthy and relatively safe. Compared to some of the cases she dealt with, where life and death were on the line, this was nothing, really.

Ella glanced at Valerie from under her eyelashes. "You know… we don't have anything else to do. We've been getting to know each other for weeks now. Perhaps we should use this time to get to know each other on a more… intimate level."

Valerie's breath caught in her throat. "I don't think that's a good idea."

"Are you sure?" Ella got onto her knees, pushing Valerie's legs apart and settling between them. She pressed a hand to Valerie's groin, putting divine pressure on Valerie's clit with the heel of her palm.

Valerie couldn't help herself. She moaned and let her head lean back against the side of the elevator. Her legs came further apart without her permission.

Ella took this as encouragement and changed her palm for her fingers. She was too low at first, but she wriggled around, watching Valerie's face in reaction to her movements.

"Ah, *fuck!*"

Ella had found Valerie's clit through her scrubs and panties. Valerie panted harshly as Ella started rubbing her. She had never been so turned on in her life and Ella had barely touched her yet. She was going to come. Oh dear god, she was going to come right now and she wasn't ready for this to end yet.

"Ella, wait."

Ella pulled back, pouting. "Do you really want me to stop."

"Hell, no. I just want fewer clothes."

Ella grinned and stripped at once. Valerie

couldn't take her eyes off Ella's body. Her full breasts, the lovely curve of her hips. Her pubic hair. Valerie pulled her own scrubs off and pulled Ella back between her legs. Their lips met in a passionate kiss. Valerie pressed her tongue into Ella's mouth and Ella easily granted her access. Their tongues twined in the most delicious dance as they pressed their bodies against each other.

Valerie reached down to brush her fingers over Ella's nipples. They hardened under her touch and Ella moaned into the kiss. Valerie took one nipple between forefinger and thumb and started rolling it gently but firmly.

Not one to be outdone, Ella put a hand back between Valerie's legs and found her clit again.

The feeling of Ella's fingers against her bare clit sent a jolt of electricity through Valerie's whole body.

"Yes, Ella, yes! Oh, fuck, just like that!" Ella was rubbing in quick, firm circles, just like Valerie did when she was touching herself, except Ella's fingers felt better than anything she'd ever done to herself.

"You look so hot like this," Ella murmured, breaking away from the kiss to speak. "I've seen how frustrated you've been, Valerie. How long has it been since you had sex? Since you even got yourself off?"

"Weeks," Valerie gasped. "Haven't touched myself in weeks. Sex, not in years."

"You poor thing. You must be so desperate." Ella pulled her hand back, grinning teasingly. "I wonder how long I could edge you before tipping you over the edge."

"No," Valerie moaned. "Ella, I need to come. Get your fingers back on me, and I mean right now."

"So bossy. Well, if you insist."

Ella started rubbing Valerie's clit, but much slower than before. It was so, so good, but not quite enough to get Valerie over the edge. Ella's fingers were sending tendrils of pleasure deep through her clit and tingling through her entire body. Heat was spreading through her pelvis and her thighs were as tense as drawn bowstrings as she hovered on the edge of orgasm.

"Ella, I need to come!" Valerie cried urgently. She felt like she might go crazy if Ella kept her on the edge like this much longer. In response, Ella took her hand away completely. Valerie felt like she could cry. She was so close and so turned on, she knew just one firm touch would send her over the edge, but Ella was denying her that.

"I'm going to make you come, Valerie. I'm going to make you come so hard you'll remember it when you're an old woman... but first, you're going to get me off with your tongue."

Valerie had been trying to suppress the thought of having her tongue on Ella for weeks. Now that it was a real possibility, she didn't hesitate. "Lie back, then."

Ella immediately did as Valerie asked, and Valerie wasted no time in spreading her legs and licking her from her pussy to her clit. Ella was soaking wet and she tasted delicious. It had been ages since Valerie had had sex with anyone, but she could swear that no one had ever tasted as good as Ella did.

Ella cried out and arched up under Valerie's tongue as Valerie flicked it over her clit. She was a bit out of practice, but she used to be good at this, and it was all coming back to her quickly. She listened carefully for Ella's reactions and adjusted accordingly.

She was soon licking Ella with abandon, going firm and fast for a few strokes before flicking her tongue lightly over the tip of Ella's clit for several seconds and then repeating.

Ella writhed and moaned beneath her, grabbing Valerie by the hair and guiding her a little to the left. It was the hottest thing Valerie had ever seen.

Ella came without warning, her cry reverberating around the small space as her legs tensed up and her hips came right up off the floor.

Valerie kept licking her until Ella weakly pushed her head away, panting. Valerie's body was screaming for its own release, but she forced herself to give Ella time to recover. Fortunately, Ella didn't seem to need long. As soon as she had her breath back, she was pushing Valerie into a sitting position and once more pressing her hand between Valerie's legs.

Valerie was already so close, she knew it wasn't going to take long to get her there, but Ella was once more going so agonizingly slow that she thought she might die of unrealized desire before she achieved release.

"Tell me how much you need this, Valerie. Tell me how desperate you are."

Valerie was past holding into any dregs of dignity. "I need it so bad, Ella. I'm going to explode.

My body is on fire. I have to come. You have to make me come. Please. I need it now. I can't wait anymore. Oh, fuck, Ella, just there, right there! Please, Ella, faster. I have to—I've got to come..."

Valerie descended into incoherent babbling as Ella finally, finally started moving her hand faster.

"I'm going to come, Ella! Oh god, I'm coming *now!*"

"Come for me, Valerie. Let go."

Valerie came, practically sobbing with relief as her orgasm took her breath away. Her entire body shook with it as she clenched her legs around Ella's hand. Ella kept rubbing firm and fast, riding Valerie through it.

Valerie felt herself squirting, and she couldn't stop it. She had never squirted before, and in a public elevator didn't seem like the best place to start, but she couldn't help herself. Her pussy gushed as Ella's continued rubbing drew out her orgasm impossibly long, until Valerie thought she may die from sheer pleasure before it ended.

When it finally did, Valerie collapsed heavily against the side of the elevator, gasping for breath. Ella removed her hand and came to sit next to Valerie, who was still in a heap on the floor.

"Does that feel better?"

"You know it does, Ella. No need to be smug."

"You don't need to deny yourself, Valerie. It's not good for you."

Valerie shrugged. She was still processing what had just happened. It had been years since she'd had sex, and when she had, it hadn't been with an employee, let alone in a workplace. Sex may not be a big deal with Ella, but it was to Valerie.

She knew that she shouldn't have done it, but she was practically lightheaded from relief and release and couldn't bring herself to regret it right now. Maybe she would later, but for now, all she could feel was relaxed and sated.

Perhaps now she wouldn't struggle so much with her attraction to Ella. She'd gotten to experience all of her dirtiest fantasies, the one she denied even to herself, and she was beyond satisfied with the outcome.

Surely, she wouldn't struggle so much anymore.

By the time they were rescued from the elevator, Valerie and Ella were dressed, and they had used Ella's spare scrub cap to mop up the mess Valerie had made.

"I'm sorry," Valerie mumbled. "I'll wash the scrub cap for you."

"Don't worry about it, I can wash it myself. Besides, it was hot as hell." Ella winked at her, putting the scrub cap in her pocket.

To Valerie's utter indignation, the experience in the elevator didn't make things easier on her.

If anything, it made them worse. It was like now that her body had gotten a taste of what being with Ella felt like, it was demanding more so relentlessly that Valerie was having a hard time focusing on anything else.

She knew that it was irrational to be angry with Ella, but she was. Why did Ella have to be so damn irresistible? Valerie was trying, she really was, but Ella was like a walking sex goddess and Valerie felt like she was a hapless moth being drawn toward a flame.

Her phone rang, jolting her out of her irritated thoughts. "What?" Valerie answered impatiently.

"Valerie, it's Ella. I'm at the diner. Are we still on for lunch today?"

"No, we're not," Valerie snapped. "I'm a busy woman, Ella, and I can't devote all my time to you."

"Oh. I—were you pulled into a surgery?"

"I've got a lot of paperwork to do. I'll see you later, Ella."

Valerie hung up, grumbling to herself. She

knew she wasn't being fair to Ella, but she also knew that lunch with Ella right now would be a bad, bad idea. She was about ninety-percent certain that the two of them would end up in the nearest bathroom screwing each other's brains out.

She couldn't have that. Valerie sternly reminded herself that it was against hospital rules, and when you broke the rules, people died. She of all people should remember that.

11

ELLA

Ella was thoroughly vexed. It had been a week since the hot elevator sex, and Valerie had been as disagreeable as a cat in a sack since then. She would have thought that some good sex would loosen Valerie up, but no, Valerie had been giving her the cold shoulder ever since.

Ella wondered if she had made a mistake initiating things with Valerie. It seemed to have put back their progress significantly, but she couldn't bring herself to regret the elevator sex. It was hands-down the best sex she'd ever had. Seeing Valerie come apart like that under her touch was the hottest thing Ella had ever been witness to.

Well, Ella wasn't giving up that easily. Valerie may not want to have sex again—her loss—but Ella wasn't going to give up on their budding friendship. She would talk to Valerie and clear all this up. There was no problem so bad it didn't have a solution. She would fix this.

So, she went up to Valerie's office and knocked.

"Not now. Please come back later."

Ella hesitated. Valerie didn't sound good. Was she crying? Should Ella leave or should she check on Valerie to make sure she was okay?

The urge to check on her won out. She stepped into the office, closing the door quietly behind her.

"Valerie?"

Valerie was sitting at her desk with her head in her hands. She looked up to reveal that she was indeed crying. "Go away, Ella."

"I'm not going anywhere." Ella came around the desk, pulling up a chair to sit beside Valerie. "What's wrong? What happened?"

"It's nothing."

"It's clearly not. You may as well just tell me, because I'm not leaving until I'm sure you're okay."

"Why do you have to be stubborn?"

"Because I care about you, Valerie. You can talk to me."

Valerie sighed. "It's... His name is Tommy. *Was* Tommy. He was only seven. I've been trying to save him since he was a toddler. He had so many surgeries. I've seldom seen cardiomyopathy that bad, let alone in a child. I fought tooth and nail to save him, but in the end, it was all for naught. He died on my table an hour ago."

"Oh, Valerie, I'm so sorry."

Tears fell thick and fast from Valerie's eyes even as she tried to swipe them away. "I should be stronger than this. Patients die. It happens."

"That doesn't mean you can't be heartbroken by it."

Valerie let out a strangled sob. Ella pulled Valerie's head onto her shoulder, rubbing her back as Valerie cried. It was so uncharacteristic to see Valerie break down like this. This vulnerability was a side of her that Ella hadn't seen before.

Of course, she had known that Valerie must have had her bad days and her struggles, but she was honored that Valerie felt comfortable enough to share it with her. Valerie could have kicked Ella out of her office. A few weeks ago, she simply would have called security should Ella have refused to leave.

Valerie's tears eventually slowed and she

pulled back, wiping her eyes. "I'm sorry. That was unprofessional. I'm your boss—"

"You're my friend as well, Valerie. Being a shoulder to cry on is part of what friends do. There's no rule against that," Ella added with a smile.

That got a small smile out of Valerie. "No, I suppose there isn't. Thank you, Ella."

Valerie took Ella by complete surprise by leaning forward and pressing a soft kiss to her lips. By the shocked expression on her face, it looked like Valerie had taken herself by surprise too. Ella wanted to kiss her until Valerie forgot all of her sorrows, but she didn't want to take advantage of Valerie while she was feeling vulnerable, so she resisted.

Instead, she asked the question that had been rolling around in her head for a while now. "Would you like to come out with me?"

Valerie tensed. "We go out all the time, Ella."

The last week notwithstanding, though neither of them mentioned that.

"That's not what I mean. I meant come out with me on a date."

Ella could practically see the shutters closing

behind Valerie's eyes. "I'm sorry, Ella, but that's against hospital policy."

Ella wanted to protest—Valerie was the one who wrote the policy, for fuck's sake—but Valerie was still looking tearful and Ella knew that though she had stopped crying, Tommy's death was still on her mind.

"Okay, Valerie. I'll see you later, then." Ella got up and left. She went into the stairwell and kicked the railing, trying to relieve her feelings.

It would be one thing if Valerie didn't want to go out with her. That, Ella could accept. But Valerie was turning her down based on a stupid *rule?* Ella had to admit, she was pissed that Valerie would turn away from their obvious connection for such a minor reason.

After all, it was hardly like other hospital employees didn't have relationships under the radar. Ella supposed that it would be a little different for Valerie, being the boss, but who's to say she couldn't change her policy?

Ella cared about Valerie a lot, but her blind adherence to rules drove Ella crazy. She understood that Valerie had some trauma around rules, but had she never heard of working through trauma? She could go to therapy rather than try to hold everyone else to her ridiculous standards.

As much as she liked Valerie, she was one of the most infuriating people Ella had ever met.

12

VALERIE

Once again, Valerie found herself thinking about Ella. She supposed that thinking about Ella was better than thinking about Tommy, but it was an exercise in frustration rather than one in grief.

Ella had been stiff and off with her ever since that day in the office—ever since Valerie had turned her down for the date. Valerie thought it was rather immature, giving her the cold shoulder just because the rules forbade them from dating. It wasn't like Valerie could very well go making exceptions for herself to the rules she had written.

Well, if Ella was going to be stubborn about this, then Valerie could be stubborn right back.

She wasn't going to break the rules, not for Ella, not for anyone. She missed her daily lunches with Ella, but she was just going to have to deal with that until Ella got her head out of her ass.

The week passed slowly. Valerie loved her job, but without lunch with Ella to look forward to, she seemed to take less enjoyment in everything. As much as she was annoyed with Ella, she couldn't stop thinking about her.

Having sex had been a big deal for Valerie. She had forgotten how good it could be—not just the physical pleasure part—but being that close to another person. She wanted it again, and she wanted it with Ella.

She couldn't have that, though. It was against the rules, and the thought of trying to find someone else outside of the hospital to date held no appeal to her.

The week took a turn for the worse when a grieving patient's family opened a lawsuit against Dr. Roth. He hadn't done anything wrong but trying to explain that to the family of the patient who died on his table wasn't going well.

Valerie eventually gave up on negotiations and handed the entire mess over to their lawyers.

On Friday afternoon, she walked out of yet

another long meeting between Dr. Roth, hospital legal representation and herself, thoroughly frustrated. She wanted someone to vent to, and Ella was the first person who came to mind.

Maybe Ella was being stupid about the whole dating thing, but Valerie couldn't think of anyone she wanted to talk to more right now. She hesitated for a moment before pulling out her phone and navigating to Ella's number. Ella answered promptly, as she always did.

"Hi, Valerie. What's up?"

"I was wondering if you wanted to come over to my place tonight, Ella? I could make us dinner."

Valerie was already having second thoughts about this. She and Ella had barely spoken for a week. Ella was bound to say no.

"I'd love to. Does seven work?"

It took Valerie a moment to respond, not having expected Ella's answer. "Yes, seven is perfect. I'll see you then, Valerie."

"See you then."

Valerie hung up, her mood suddenly much improved.

Ella arrived at exactly seven, quite a feat given how unpredictable both of their jobs could be. She must have made an effort to shift things around so that she didn't have any surgeries that were likely to run overtime at the end of the day.

She had showered and changed out of her scrubs. Her hair was still slightly wet, and she was wearing jeans and a red t-shirt that hugged her breasts in a way that threatened to drive Valerie to distraction.

"Please, come in. I've made us a casserole."

"That sounds perfect." Ella smiled at Valerie, a smile that made Valerie want to kiss her so badly, it felt like an ache in her chest.

Valerie led her inside. Ella sat down while Valerie served up dinner.

"So, what made you decide to break the wall of silence and invite me here?"

Valerie shrugged. "I had a bad week. I needed someone to talk to. You were the only one who came to mind."

"My week hasn't been great either, Valerie. I don't like not talking to you."

"Well, maybe you shouldn't have gotten all offended that I don't want to date you. It's quite immature, Ella, and frankly, it's beneath you."

Ella raised an eyebrow. "Is that what you think?"

"What do you mean?"

"Valerie, if I really thought you said no because you genuinely didn't want to date me, there would be no issues between us. I would be disappointed, sure, but I would get over it. I'm pissed because I can tell that you *do* want to give it a shot, but you're throwing that shot away because of a stupid rule."

And here it was. Ella's disregard for the rules, slapping Valerie in the face once more.

"It's not stupid," Valerie growled. "Relationships lead to personal drama, and when people are involved in their personal dramas rather than their work, patients die. That's what breaking the rules does, Ella—it kills people."

Valerie expected Ella to argue. She was sure that this would turn into a screaming match that would ultimately end in Ella storming out.

Ella, however, took a moment before responding. "I get your perspective, Valerie. I know that the rules are there for a reason, and I know that a lot of those rules were put into place because patients died. I realize that you're just trying to protect your patients. I've got a different view, though. Can I explain it to you?"

This wasn't the confrontation she had been expecting and it threw Valerie off. She thought about it and decided that it couldn't hurt to hear Ella's point of view. Even if it was wrong, that didn't mean she shouldn't try to listen to understand Ella better.

"Yeah, okay."

"I've seen more patients than I can count die because their insurance wouldn't cover their treatment, all because the terms of service excluded the surgery they needed for some reason. I've seen too many patients die or live permanently disabled because the surgeons I worked under wouldn't approve the experimental procedures that could have saved them.

"You say that breaking rules kills patients, and you are right in some cases, but in my experience, sticking too rigidly to rules, especially unnecessary rules, also kills them. If we want to do our best for our patients, we need to find some middle ground between rigidity and anarchy."

Valerie could see Ella's point. She had been on the receiving end of insurance nightmares enough times to know how heartbreaking it was to see patients turned away for financial reasons. And while she wouldn't bend the rules to allow for unapproved procedures, she couldn't deny that those procedures did save a lot of lives.

"I suppose I can understand that. I'm not saying I can condone you breaking the rules, but I guess I can see your perspective a little."

"That's all I'm asking, Valerie. I think if we can understand each other a bit better, we'll do just fine."

Valerie wasn't so sure, but she couldn't help but be caught up in Ella's optimism. It felt good to be on speaking terms with Ella again. She was glad that she had misunderstood Ella's previous silence after her refusal on the dating issue.

The conversation turned to lighter things, and Valerie's spirits lifted. She loved talking to Ella. Just being near her was a balm to the ragged edges of her mind.

When dinner ended, Ella and Valerie got up at the same time.

"What are you doing?"

"I'm helping you wash up."

"No way. You're a guest. I'll do the washing up later tonight."

Ella rolled her eyes. "I'm not leaving you with a pile of dishes that's going to keep you up late tonight and make you exhausted tomorrow, Valerie. Stop being stubborn and let me help."

With that, Ella marched into the kitchen and picked up a scrubbing brush.

"See who's being stubborn now," Valerie muttered, but she wasn't really annoyed. Ella was right about the big pile of dishes. Valerie really needed to get a housekeeper, but she felt wary of inviting a stranger into her space.

Valerie joined Ella at the sink and started drying and putting away the dishes as Ella washed them. Their elbows bumped every now and then, and as they finished, they both turned to face each other but underestimated exactly how close they were together, bringing themselves practically chest to chest.

Valerie knew she should step back, but her feet didn't seem to want to cooperate with her brain's commands. Instead, her body did the exact opposite of what she was telling it. She found herself wrapping an arm around Ella's neck and drawing her closer.

Ella offered no resistance, and in a mere moment, they were kissing.

Either Valerie had forgotten how good kissing Ella was, or the time apart had only made the kisses that much sweeter. Ella moaned into the kiss and Valerie took the opportunity to press her tongue inside Ella's mouth.

It seemed that Ella had the same idea, resulting in an awkward battle of advancing tongues for a few moments before they slid past each other and settled easily into the kiss.

Valerie grabbed Ella's hips, never breaking the kiss, and settled her on the counter. She pressed a hand between Ella's legs, pressing the heel of her hand down over her clit through her clothes.

Ella broke away from the kiss, gasping and rocking her hips forward slightly. Valerie smiled triumphantly and struggled with the zipper to Ella's jeans for a moment before getting it undone and sliding her hand inside Ella's panties. She started touching Ella's clitoris, which she could feel responding to her as she re-captured her mouth in a scorching kiss.

Ella wrapped her arms around Valerie's neck and hung on for dear life. She spread her legs and tilted her hips, giving Valerie the best access she could in the current position. Valerie remembered what Ella had done to her and repeated the same movements on Ella.

It turned out that she was right in her guess

that Ella had done the same to Valerie as she liked to do to herself, because with minutes, Ella was a wet, writhing mess beneath Valerie's fingers.

"Valerie, I—oh fuck, yes please, like that—we should go to the bedroom."

"Why go to the bedroom when there's a perfectly good counter right here?"

Valerie had to admit that she had a bit of a sadistic urge to get back at Ella for teasing her so thoroughly in the elevator. Let's see how Ella reacted to being thoroughly destroyed.

She grabbed Ella's hips again and spun her around, setting her feet on the floor and bending her over the counter. She pressed two fingers into Ella's soaked pussy, curling them to get her G-spot.

Ella made a muffled sound of encouragement and thrust her hips back, her face pressed into one of her arms.

Valerie started thrusting, adding a third finger, filling Ella up, relishing in the feeling of Ella's slick pussy contracting around her fingers.

Ella was crying out and pushing back onto Valerie's fingers, but she wasn't quite there yet. Valerie had an idea and pulled her fingers out, ignoring Ella's whine of protest. "Wait here."

"But Valerie—"

"I said wait."

Valerie hurried through to her bedroom and grabbed her favorite butterfly vibrator from the drawer before returning to Ella.

"Lift your hips a little. There you go."

Ella let out a strangled gasp as Valerie fitted the butterfly over her clit and turned it on. She repositioned Ella's hips carefully, putting the butterfly directly on the counter's edge, giving Ella the perfect leverage to grind it onto her clit.

Ella took advantage of the position at once, riding the counter with abandon. Valerie re-inserted her fingers, twisting them to stroke Ella's G-spot.

Ella's cries became short and choppy, and Valerie saw her legs tensing.

She removed her fingers and with her other hand, used the remote to turn the vibrator off.

"*Valerie!*"

"Patience, Ella. You can wait a bit longer for me, can't you?"

"I can't!" Ella wailed. "I have to come!"

"Funny, I said much the same thing. I recall you making me wait anyway."

"Please, Valerie. Please, I have to come."

Ella started grinding against the counter again, but Valerie grabbed her hips, holding her back.

"Tell me how desperate you are, Ella."

See how the tables had turned.

"I'm desperate, Valerie! I need this. I'm so close. One stray breath of wind will push me over the edge. I'm right on the edge and it's killing me. Oh god, I'm going to die if I don't come right now!"

Valerie wanted to say something witty about how it was physically impossible to die of desire, but seeing Ella in such a state of dire arousal was doing things to her and she found she couldn't wait any longer.

She wanted to see Ella come, and she wanted it now.

So, she turned on the toy and pushed her fingers back into Ella's pussy.

The moment Valerie's fingers entered her, less than two seconds after the vibrator had come on again, Ella came. She screamed, grinding hard into the counter, her hands clutching at the other side as she squirted noisily onto the tiled floor.

Valerie battered Ella's G-spot relentlessly through her whole orgasm, drawing it out as long as possible.

She knew it was over when Ella's knees gave

away and she started sliding off the counter and onto the floor. Valerie chuckled as she caught Ella's hips, turning and lifting her back up on the countertop.

Ella flopped back, lying on the counter with her legs hanging off, her pussy glistening wet and so very tempting.

Valerie was already sticking her hand into her own pants, rubbing frantically on her clit. She was almost as desperate as Ella had been and she wasn't going to wait any longer.

"Wait. Let me do that."

"I can't wait," Valerie gasped.

Ella slid off the counter and went smoothly to her knees. She undid Valerie's pants and pulled them down to her ankles, finally removing Valerie's hand.

Valerie scarcely had time to complain, because as soon as her fingers were pulled away, they were replaced with Ella's tongue.

And *oh,* Ella's tongue was so much better than Valerie's fingers had been. She braced herself against the dishwasher and spread her legs, giving Ella better access.

It seemed that Ella had decided not to torture her this time, because she licked quickly and firmly in a relentless rhythm that soon pushed Valerie to her release.

She clutched at the dishwasher as her orgasm overtook her, threatening to buckle her legs like Ella's had.

Ella kept licking her, bringing the orgasm up to even greater heights. Valerie came and came, until she was unsure if it would ever end. She may not be squirting this time, but this was the longest and most intense orgasm she had ever had.

It went on for so long that she started to get lightheaded from lack of oxygen and was forced to draw in an urgent breath as pleasure continued to bombard her. The orgasm finally ended, leaving Valerie limp in its wake. She sank to the floor beside Ella, who grinned at her.

"No need to look so smug."

"Why shouldn't I? I just gave you the best orgasm of your life, didn't I?"

"Who's to say that it was?" Valerie challenged. "I'm a lot older than you, you know."

"And yet, I seem to have more experience, what with the way you've cut yourself off from relationships. Admit it, you've never had anything better than that."

"I haven't," Valerie admitted reluctantly. "Your

tongue is fucking magic. We have to do that again sometime."

Ella looked up at her, surprise written across her flushed, sweaty face. "Really?"

Valerie sighed. She shouldn't be saying this, but was there really any point in denying it anymore?

"I just can't seem to resist you," she admitted. "I've been fighting and fighting it, but I'm tired of fighting."

"And if it's against the rules?"

"Don't remind me," Valerie moaned, covering her face with one hand. "I'm such a hypocrite."

"You do know that other people have relationships in the workplace, right?"

"I know they try, but I shut it down whenever I catch wind of it. What? Why are you laughing?"

"You don't shut anything down, Valerie. You just make people sneakier."

"*What?*"

"Did you really think you could successfully tell anyone who to love? You should know that never works."

"Do you mean to tell me that people are having secret against-the-rules relationships right now without my knowledge?"

Ella nodded, her lips twitching. "Sorry to be the one to break it to you."

"This—this is unacceptable!" Valerie spluttered. "Who is breaking the rules in this manner?"

"Well, you and me, for starters."

That brought Valerie up short. Ella had a point there. What right did she have to judge others for breaking the rules when she was doing the exact same thing?

"I... Well, I suppose I can't rightfully go after them when I... Well, shit."

Ella chuckled. "Really, Valerie, we should be honoring the spirit of the rule rather than the letter of it. Why did you create that rule in the first place?"

"To prevent personal relationships from interfering with people's work," Valerie said at once.

"So as long as we don't let this interfere with our work, what's the problem?"

"Can we stop it from messing with our work, though? Is it really possible to separate feelings like that?"

"People have successful workplace relationships all the time. If they can do it, so can we."

Valerie thought carefully about what she

wanted to say next. The last thing she wanted was to hurt Ella's feelings, but she had to be honest.

"Ella, we can't be in a relationship. Not in the sense of romance. Sex, yes, but it can't be anything more than that."

Ella lifted her chin. "Why not?"

She clearly expected Valerie to cite the rules again, but that actually wasn't what Valerie was worried about right now. "You may be confident in your ability to separate your feelings well enough not to compromise patient care, but I'm not. If we were in a relationship and something happened between us, I can't guarantee I could work effectively with you when a patient's life is on the line. People could die, Ella. I can't risk it. Plus, I am twenty years older than you. It would never work."

"I didn't hear in any of that that you don't want it."

Valerie did want it but admitting that to Ella wouldn't help anything. "I don't want to risk it, Ella. I won't have patients dying because of decisions I make in my personal life."

"You can't let your job hold your personal life hostage."

Valerie raised an eyebrow. "Oh, really? And when was the last time you socialized with anyone outside of work, or did anything non-work related on one of your off days?"

Ella blushed. "That's different. I love my work."

"And you think I don't love mine? We've both made many sacrifices for our careers and will continue to do so. I'm very selfish. I've always been basically single and it has been very successful for me. I don't have any intention of changing that now. This is all I can give, Ella. The question is, will it be enough for you?"

Valerie was more invested than she wanted to admit in Ella saying yes. Not only did she want the sex—and she *really* wanted the sex—but she wanted the closeness and intimacy that came with it. She was only realizing now how lonely she really was, and her proposition to Ella seemed like the perfect solution.

She and Ella enjoyed each other's company, and they were certainly physically compatible. All she'd have to do would be to make sure her feelings didn't switch from friendship to romance, and everything would be perfect.

There was a long pause before Ella responded, during which Valerie waited nervously.

"Yes. Yes, that will be enough for me. As long as

we can be friends as well; I hate fighting with you, Valerie."

Valerie let out a slow breath of relief. "I also definitely want to maintain our friendship. We're agreed, then? Friends with benefits?"

"Friends with benefits," Ella agreed.

They leaned in and sealed their agreement with a kiss.

13

ELLA

"You ask her."

"No, you."

"No way."

"I'll do it," Stephanie finally whispered to the gaggle of nurses around her. She walked over to Ella and leaned against the counter, clearly trying to appear casual, but Ella wasn't fooled. "Hi, Ella."

"Hey, Stephanie. Was there something I could help you with?"

"Are you and Doctor Bush dating?" Stephanie blurted out.

"No."

Stephanie narrowed her eyes suspiciously. "Are

you sure? Because I was sure I saw you wearing her sweater yesterday."

Ella hadn't thought anyone would notice, but apparently, she'd been wrong. She really needed to start leaving clothes at Valerie's house, but they had been avoiding taking that step. It was a step for couples, after all, not friends with benefits, which —Ella had to keep reminding herself—was what they were.

She wondered whether she should lie, but the thought sat wrong with her. On the other hand, she knew Valerie wouldn't be impressed if she just spilled their secret to the nurses. If it got out, it would spread through the hospital like wildfire.

"We're not *dating*," Ella said carefully. "We're good friends, though. *Very* good friends." She looked intently at Stephanie, hoping she would understand.

"Oh. *Oh.* I see. Well, I'll... I just need to finish some charts."

Despite her question, Stephanie clearly hadn't been expecting Ella to admit—or imply—that she and Valerie were anything more than colleagues. Ella just hoped the rumors didn't reach Valerie.

There was a good chance they wouldn't. Valerie was such as stickler for rules that people had learned to keep rumors away from her ears, lest they get into trouble.

Ella watched Stephanie go back to report to the other nurses and couldn't help but feel disappointed. She couldn't deny it to herself. Though she and Valerie weren't dating, Ella wished it was otherwise.

She had wanted to date Valerie from the start, but it was different now. Ella had had every intention to honor the agreement she had made with Valerie—to remain no more than friends. However, her heart had other ideas.

She was falling for Valerie and falling hard. Every day, Ella dug herself deeper into this pit, and she didn't know how to get out.

The worst was that she was sure Valerie felt the same. She could see it in the way Valerie looked at her, feel it in the way Valerie touched her.

Maybe things were different for Valerie now, just like they were for Ella. It couldn't hurt to ask, right?

Yeah, that's what she was going to do. She'd just ask Valerie out on a date. Nice and easy. The worst thing Valerie could do was say no. Ella could live with that.

She was nervous when lunch time came. She

and Valerie had picked up their habit of having lunches together again and met at the diner as usual.

"Hey, beautiful." Valerie pressed an easy kiss to Ella's lips before sitting down. "What happened to you? Are you waiting to hear back from insurance for a patient or something?"

Ella focussed on Valerie's lovely brown eyes which were usually warm now when they looked at her instead of the cold hard eyes she had been met with so much at the start.

Strands of greying dark blonde hair had escaped around her face. She looked tired.

"No. I just wanted to ask you something."

"Fire away."

"I want to take you on a date—a real date. I know we have these lunches, but these are just as friends. I want to go on something that we both agree is a date, as more than friends. I want to be more than your friend, Valerie."

Valerie's face fell. "You know we can't, Ella. We're already breaking the rules by even sleeping together. Being in a relationship... It's too far across the line. It is too risky for me. I'm sorry."

Well, it turned out Ella had been wrong. It *could* hurt to ask, and she didn't think she could live with Valerie saying no. She felt tears threatening and leaped up. "I'm sorry, but I'm not feeling well. I think I need to take the rest of the day off work. I'll see you tomorrow, Valerie."

With that, she dashed out.

Ella tried to stop the stupid tears, but they wouldn't cooperate. She was such an idiot. Of course Valerie had said no. Valerie was too entrenched in her stupid rules to make an exception, even for Ella. Clearly, she didn't care for Ella as much as Ella had hoped she did.

Ella went home and tried to talk herself out of her growing misery. She should have known this would happen. She had put her heart on the line, hoping Valerie would change the rules for her, but in hindsight, that was a crazy hope. She remembered what Valerie had told her all those weeks ago.

I am not changing the rules. Not for you; not for anyone.

Well, she certainly was consistent.

Through her tears and hurt, Ella realized that she couldn't keep doing this. She couldn't deny any longer that she wanted more from Valerie, and Valerie had made it clear that Ella wasn't going to get it from her.

As much as she wanted to go back to Valerie and tell her that they could just continue as they had been, Ella knew that it would only hurt her in the long run. She would only fall harder for Valerie, and Valerie would retreat further behind the rules she liked to hold so close around herself.

No, it would never work. Ella couldn't do that to herself. She deserved more than to be in a relationship that didn't truly fulfill her.

So, with a sinking heart, she picked up her phone and messaged Valerie.

Hi, Valerie. So I've been doing some thinking, and I've decided that I can't keep doing this. I know I originally said that friends with benefits would be enough for me, and I truly thought it would be, but things have changed. I want you to be more than a friend, and you can't give me that. I'm not going to hurt us both by staying in a relationship where we both want different things.

I think it would be best if from now on we could remain just colleagues. I hope you can understand, and I trust that you won't let this affect our work together.

. . .

Valerie read the message within a few minutes but didn't respond. Well, she had read it, and that's all that mattered. Ella couldn't quite suppress a stupid hope that Valerie would call, telling Ella she'd changed her mind, that she wanted to give dating a try, but she never did.

Ella went to bed alone and cried herself to sleep, wishing more than anything that things could be different.

14

VALERIE

Valerie knew this sick, sinking feeling. It was the same feeling she got when a patient was crashing because she hadn't picked the correct course of treatment, when she knew that it was too late and she would lose them.

It was the feeling she got when she knew she had made a terrible mistake.

She stared at Ella's message, trying to rationalize the feeling away. She couldn't have made a mistake. She was acting according to the rules.

Honestly, it was probably for the best. She and Ella had been breaking the rules for weeks now in the most delicious ways, and if they hadn't been,

Valerie wouldn't be feeling like this right now. She should never have started this thing with Ella. If she had never started it, then she would never have started falling for her.

How could she be falling for someone so much younger than her? Someone so different from her.

She thought maybe it was just a lust thing. Ella's dazzling looks and the incredible sex they had together. That kind of thing made people crazy, right? That was the kind of thing that got mistaken for love all the time.

But it wasn't love, was it? It was just serious chemistry between two people making them think it was more.

That was all it was between her and Ella, right? Serious chemistry masquerading as more?

But Valerie couldn't help thinking maybe it was more in this case.

They might be so different in so many ways, but in their focus on their careers and their drive to save lives, they were very much the same.

Every little thing Ella did just made Valerie fall a little bit more in love with her. It was like Ella was a flame and Valerie was a hapless moth.

It wasn't just Ella's lovely body and almost magical eyes, was it?

As much as Ella frustrated her, Valerie couldn't help but respect the way Ella fiercely fought for what was right. Every other doctor and nurse and other staff that had worked beneath Valerie always did as Valerie commanded.

Ella was the first and only to stand up to her. Ella's changes to the clinic had saved hundreds of lives, Valerie was sure of it.

Ella was passionate and fearless and Valerie realized in that very moment that she loved that about her.

Valerie looked at the text again. She should respond. She should assure Ella that she wouldn't let this affect their work, but she felt frozen in place, her body not responding as it usually did.

"Dr. Bush? Earth to Dr. Valerie Bush?"

Dr. Lily Gold grabbed Valerie's hand and pulled her into one of the consultation rooms.

"Lily? What are you doing here? Shouldn't you be up in psychiatry? You have your own department to run."

"I got a very concerned call from one of your nurses, saying she thought you were going into shock. Apparently, you weren't responding to visual or auditory cues."

Crap. "I'm sorry. I guess I was just distracted."

"With what?"

"Just work stuff."

"Bullshit, Valerie. Whatever it is, you'd better spill it. Did something happen with your baby surgeon with the big ocean eyes?"

Valerie's eyes widened in shock. She hadn't told anyone about her and Ella.

"What? What makes you think—?"

"Please. You practically get hearts in your eyes when you talk about her."

Lily had known her a long time and she clearly knew her very well.

"I do not!"

"Yeah, you do. So, it's about Ocean Eyes, then?"

Valerie sighed. Maybe she did need to talk to someone, and Lily was her closest friend—apart from Ella. Were she and Ella even friends anymore?

"Ella broke things off."

"What? Why?"

"Um… she asked me on a date, and I turned her down. She left in a hurry and texted me shortly afterward. Whatever was happening, it's over between us."

"You turned her down? Hot young Ocean Eyes? What's wrong with you, Valerie? You're clearly head over heels for that woman! It has been obvious for weeks. The whole hospital knows. Go on a date with her, for goodness sake!"

"I can't. It's against the rules."

"That's a lie and you know it."

"It is not a lie! I can get you a copy of the hospital policy right now. It says in paragraph thirteen—"

"I'm not talking about the stupid hospital policy, Valerie. I'm talking about the fact that it's not the reason you don't want to date Ella."

"Of course that's the reason I don't want to date Ella. Why else wouldn't I want to? Ella is an amazing person. Anyone would be privileged to date her."

"Oh, I know. Ella Ocean Eyes is super hot stuff. She's not the problem. You are."

"Really. Why don't you enlighten me, then."

"You've let this job mess with your head, Valerie. You've become jaded. All surgeons see more than their fair share of death. You've had more hearts stop in your hands than I could even begin to count. If you let yourself truly embrace everything you and Ella could be, she will die."

"What are you talking about?"

"Probably not anytime in the near future, but

sooner or later, Ella will die, and she will leave those who love her heartbroken. You don't want to be one of those people. That's why you've really avoided relationships all these years. You fix hearts for a living, but you're afraid that yours will be broken irreparably."

Valerie opened her mouth to tell Lily that she was wrong, and then closed it again. Was she really wrong? Valerie imagined what would happen if Ella went to work at another hospital, where the rules against dating wouldn't apply to them. What would she do then?

Well, if Ella was at another hospital, their schedules probably wouldn't even match up. Dating would be impossible and— well, then there was the age gap... and ... and Valerie was just making excuses. Crap. Maybe Lily was right. Perhaps she would have taken any excuse not to date—not to put her heart on the line.

"You may have a point."

"I know I do."

"What do I do about it, then?"

"You need to make a decision, Valerie. How bad is it being lonely and alone versus how bad it would be to lose someone you love?"

Lily's pager beeped and she glanced down at it. "I've got to go. Think about it, Valerie."

"Thanks, Lily."

Valerie stared after Lily, deep in thought. Which was really worse? Living as she was or having her heart broken?

The more she thought about it, the more Valerie became convinced that her current course was the correct one. Sure, she wasn't entirely happy right now, but she was certain that what she was feeling right now was a million times better than what she would feel if she was with Ella and then lost her.

It wasn't like she was guaranteed a lifetime of happiness if she dated Ella. It could easily go wrong—a time of happiness in exchange for a lifetime of heartbreak if they broke up, or worst case, something happened to Ella.

No, it wasn't worth the risk. Valerie would focus on her work, which had always fulfilled her. That would have to be enough.

Work wasn't enough any more.

Valerie missed Ella so much it felt like a shard of glass in her vulnerable insides. She wanted what they had back. She couldn't risk being in a relationship with Ella, but they could surely at least be friends. They could at least share their bodies together and be close in that way. The intimacy had been so valuable to Valerie.

So, she resolved to seduce Ella. She knew that Ella was attracted to her. Surely, it wouldn't be that difficult.

Valerie planned it carefully. She made sure that her and Ella's schedules were both clear before calling Ella to her office.

Ella knocked and waited.

"Ella, please come in."

Ella stepped inside, watching Valerie warily. Her lovely eyes were more green than blue today and her hair was in a thick plait over her left shoulder.

"Please, sit down."

Ella sat and Valerie walked around to the door, locking it. She pulled the cord to close the blinds on the window between her office and the corridor.

"I know we've spoken before about your fantasy of being taken over my desk. Well, here is your chance." Valerie purred. Her connection with Ella had awoken the animal within her and apparently, it wouldn't go back to sleep.

She swung one leg over the chair so that she was straddling Ella's lap.

Valerie kissed Ella deeply, her hands running

down Ella's sides as Ella moaned and returned the kiss.

Valerie was just starting to think that this was going very well when Ella turned her face to the side.

"Valerie, wait. Stop."

Valerie reluctantly pulled back. "I know you want this. Don't deny it."

"I do want this, but you also know I want more than this. I'm not going to settle for less anymore, Valerie. I deserve someone who can give me everything I want, and I'm not staying in a relationship that doesn't give me that."

A small, unbiased part of her knew that Ella's point was valid, but Valerie's hurt at the outright rejection outweighed such logical thoughts. She got off Ella's lap and folded her arms. "Very well. Get out of here, Ella."

"Valerie, don't be like that. Don't be mad. I miss you. I'd like us to try to be friends, at least."

"Well, I'd like us to pick up where we left off, but we don't always get what we want, do we?"

Ella stood up. Her eyes were flashing dark green and angry. "You're being unreasonable!"

Valerie hated herself, but she couldn't stop the

response from spilling from her mouth. "No, you're being unreasonable!"

The two of them stood there for a few seconds in stalemate, glaring at each other, before Ella turned and stalked out, slamming the door behind her. It was the most awful sensation of déjà vu. Valerie didn't like it at all, but if Ella was going to be difficult about this, Valerie wasn't going to be the first one to back down.

Once more, she had that awful, sinking feeling, but she studiously ignored it. She knew what she was doing. Ella had turned Valerie's life upside down. She had convinced Valerie to go against the rules, something Valerie would never have thought herself capable of. Ella was and always had been a wild card, and Valerie *hated* wild cards.

She would do well to remember that.

15

ELLA

Ella hated fighting with Valerie, but she didn't know how she could change anything. She wasn't going to settle for less, and Valerie wasn't going to agree to more. They were at loggerheads. They were both annoyed with each other, and Valerie had taken to spending time in her office doing paperwork again, delegating her surgeries to other surgeons.

Ella was sure that Valerie was avoiding her, trying to avoid more fights. In the beginning, Ella had accepted this strategy, but no more. She wanted Valerie, and she hadn't gotten this far in life by not fighting for what she wanted.

She was going to do her very best to woo

Valerie. If her attempts failed... Well, Ella supposed she would have to move on. It wasn't a pleasant prospect, but it also wasn't one she needed to consider right now.

So, the next day, Ella turned up at Valerie's office with yellow roses. She remembered once in bed when Valerie had mentioned the yellow rose gardens she had loved walking in with her father as a child.

Valerie answered the door, her expression shifting into one of confusion when she saw what Ella had with her. Her brown eyes were lovely and open for just a second. Her face looked hopeful. "Ella, what—?"

"Come on a date with me, Valerie." Ella was determined. Ella kept getting these glimpses of the real Valerie. The Valerie she kept buried deep beneath her frosty surface.

Valerie frowned. "You know I can't."

"I think you can, and I'm going to prove it. We belong together, Valerie. You will see that sooner or later. Until you tell me you don't want me- not because of rules or age gaps or any other stupid reasons, I'm going to do everything I can to convince you of that."

Ella hesitated, wondering if Valerie would use

this opportunity to tell her to leave once and for all. If Valerie told Ella that she wanted nothing more to do with her, Ella couldn't in good conscience keep pursuing her. That would be stalkerish and wrong.

However, she didn't think that Valerie would tell her to cease and desist. She knew that Valerie really did want her. It was just her own issues holding her back.

"I can't do this right now, Ella. I've got a surgery."

Ha. That certainly wasn't a "leave me alone," which meant Ella was still free to keep trying. Surely, Valerie would soften sooner or later.

Ella smiled sweetly and backed away. Valerie's face was softer than it might have been.

Two weeks later, Ella was beginning to reconsider that opinion. Valerie's office was now full of yellow roses, she seemed happy enough to receive them but never backed down on her decision not to date Ella. She ignored the sweet notes Ella left for her in her locker, and avoided Ella as much as was humanly possible, given that they worked in the same hospital.

She was polite to Ella when she saw her and her eyes weren't so frosty but she wouldn't acquiesce to Ella's requests.

It was an icy day and Ella decided to take the train to work rather than risk driving on the frozen roads. She sat with her head leaning against the window, trying to think of a method of courtship she had not yet tried.

"Monday getting you down?"

Ella looked up to find a pretty woman sitting in the seat opposite grinning at her.

"Something like that," she mumbled.

"Yeah, it can be pretty brutal going out in this cold. I'm Kate, by the way." Kate had dark hair and eyes and a beautiful smile.

"Ella. What kind of work do you do?"

"I'm a teacher. I teach high school chemistry. How about you?"

"I'm a neurosurgeon."

"Wow, that's super cool. What an important job. No wonder you look so serious."

"It's not that. It's... Well, it's my boss. We haven't exactly been getting on well as of late."

"Ah, I know that pain. Bosses can be tricky."

"Yeah. Anyway, your job sounds cool. What's it like working with kids?"

"It's really great! Teaching has always been my passion, you know? I love kids, and I feel like I'm really making a difference in their lives this way."

Ella and Kate chatted for the rest of the train ride. Ella found herself smiling genuinely for the first time in a while. It was good to talk to someone outside of work. She and Kate hit it off at once, and Ella was sad to hear her stop announced.

"This is me. Well, it was nice meeting you, Kate."

"It was nice meeting you too, Ella. Would you... Would you like to exchange numbers? I'd love to take you out sometime."

"Out?"

"Like on a date. If you'd be interested, I mean."

Ella hesitated. On the one hand, she still had feelings for Valerie. On the other, Valerie had made it pretty clear that she wasn't going to relent and be in a real relationship with Ella. Perhaps it was about time that Ella started getting over her.

"Or not," Kate said quickly. "I mean, we could just go as friends. If you're not interested in women—"

"No, I am! I'd love to go on a date with you, Kate."

"Great!"

They exchanged numbers and arranged to meet that evening after work for dinner. Ella tucked the note she had written for Valerie carefully into her purse. She would see how things went with Kate before continuing her attempts to seduce Valerie.

Who knew? Maybe this thing with Kate could be the start of something new, without all the complications that a relationship with Valerie presented. Ella and Kate seemed to get on well without any clashing or arguing and they both agreed on what they wanted.

Surely, this was a better match than Valerie could ever be.

Ella looked forward to the date all day, and when evening came, she had just enough time to dash home, shower and change into something nice. They weren't going to a fancy restaurant, so the clothes she chose weren't overly formal, but she picked out things that were flattering and eye-catching.

Ella braved the icy roads to drive to Joy's

Kitchen, where she found Kate already waiting for her.

"Hey, Kate."

"Ella, you made it! I wasn't sure you would. You know when you meet someone on the train, you never really know where that relationship will end up going."

"I know what you mean. I wasn't sure you'd turn up either. I'm glad you did, though."

"Me too. Shall we order?"

"Yeah. I always look at the desserts first—it's the most important part of the meal, after all."

"I do the same!" Kate grinned. "I've already taken a peek. I think I'll get the chocolate mousse cake."

"Sounds delicious."

Ella perused the menu, deciding quickly on her order and focusing back on Kate. "How was your day? How were the kids?"

"Pretty good. I had to grade some tests, which is always a bit depressing, but the kids make up for the undesirable admin parts. I even appreciate the difficult ones, as they make the job interesting."

Ella nodded. She understood what Kate meant about making the job interesting. She always sought out different kinds of cases to keep her skills sharp. Of course, she had to do a lot of the more common surgeries repeatedly, but that didn't mean she couldn't fill up the gaps in her schedule with new and challenging surgeries that would help her grow as a surgeon.

Valerie had really helped with that. When she had realized how important learning and growth were to Ella, she had started putting feelers out to other hospitals, encouraging them to send challenging cases to Ella. She had done a good job of making sure that the cases that were sent weren't ones that would put Ella in a position where she felt that she had to break the rules for the good of her patient.

Valerie understood Ella in a way no one else could—in a way no one but a fellow surgeon could.

It was so much more than just the connection over their careers, though. Ella felt like Valerie *saw* her in a way no one else had before. They had a deep personal connection, even if Valerie was too afraid to accept it.

"Ella? Are you alright?"

Ella brought her focus back to Kate. Kate was a good person and would make a great partner to whoever she dated... but Ella couldn't be that person. It wouldn't be fair to her or to Kate to start dating when she was still so hung up on Valerie.

"I'm sorry, Kate," Ella said quietly. "I can't do this. I thought I could, but... I still have feelings for someone else. I wanted to get over her, but, well, I just can't."

She had expected the disappointment she saw on Kate's face. What she didn't expect was Kate's reaction.

Kate sighed and took Ella's hand over the table. "Thanks for telling me, Ella. It's better to know upfront than try to start something when your heart isn't really in it. I'd still like us to be friends, if you're up for that."

"Really?"

Ella had expected Kate to be annoyed—she would be, if someone had agreed to date her while still having feelings for someone else. Kate's reaction took her by complete surprise and just went to prove what a decent person Kate was.

"Yes, really. I feel like we have a connection, and you don't find that often."

"Are you certain friendship will be enough for you?" Ella was all too aware of the fact that when Valerie had asked her that question, she had said yes, and it turned out that she was wrong.

"I'm sure. There are plenty of other women I can date. I'm already on Tinder. I'm sure I'll find someone soon enough. I'd love to remain friends with you. I think we could be good friends, Ella."

"I think so too. I'd be honored to be your friend, Kate."

Kate squeezed Ella's hand before letting go. "Now, tell me about this person you still have feelings for. I want to know all the gory details."

Ella grinned. She found she was looking forward to confiding in Kate. Maybe Kate would have a new perspective on her problem.

"Well, her name is Valerie and she is my boss…"

16

VALERIE

Valerie clenched her hands into fists and stomped past Ella. Ella was sitting with that pretty brunette again. They were chatting and laughing together, leaning over the tabletop toward each other.

Valerie was going crazy with jealousy. Of course, she had no grounds to complain. She couldn't expect Ella to wait around pining for her forever, especially when Valerie had told her over and over again that she didn't want to date.

Ella had every right to date and to bring her new girlfriend into the hospital cafeteria for lunch.

That didn't mean that it didn't drive Valerie crazy.

Valerie stopped in a nearby bathroom, trying to get control of herself. She needed to get her head straight before this started to affect her work. She couldn't drive herself crazy thinking about another woman's hands on Ella's body.

It should be *her* hands and no one else's. No one else should get to touch her Ella.

No. That's exactly the kind of thought that would send her into a jealous rage and have her storming over to Ella's girlfriend and doing something she would sorely regret later.

She went to her office, which was more and more becoming her sanctuary nowadays. She hated that she was avoiding surgery simply to avoid Ella, but she knew that if she got pulled into a surgery with Ella now, she would start interrogating her about her new girlfriend, and that conversation would absolutely end in an argument.

Over an operating table was not a good time, so for now, Valerie was avoiding surgeries, at least until she could get her emotions under control.

She stayed late that night, knowing that Ella would leave at five and not wanting to bump into her. Valerie was therefore surprised when she nearly collided with Ella on her way to the locker room. Ella was dressed in a surgical gown and practically jumped out of her skin when she saw Valerie.

"Valerie! What are you doing here so late?"

"I was working." Valerie narrowed her eyes. "What are *you* doing here so late?"

"I... um..."

"Ella, why do you have a surgical gown on? You don't have any surgeries scheduled for this evening."

"Look, don't be mad, okay?"

"What did you do?"

"You know that patient who I was supposed to send home because of legal issues? Well... I kind of didn't. He needed that surgery."

"Ella, under no circumstances are you to perform that surgery. He's mentally unstable and a ward of the state. The state did not approve the surgery. Operating on him would be as good as operating on a patient without their consent!"

"You know as well as I do that the people in charge of those approvals don't really care about whether he lives or dies. They just don't want the extra work of caring for someone after a big surgery."

Valerie knew the harsh truth of that. She knew that the state-care facilities were stretched to the breaking point, but that was no reason to sit back and let people die. Still, rules were rules. They had to follow their legal team's advice, and their legal team had said to send him home.

"The answer is no, Ella."

Ella lifted her chin. "It's too late. The surgery is already done. He's in recovery right now."

"ELLA! Do you have any idea how much trouble the hospital could get into over that? Do you even care?"

"Of course I care about the hospital, Valerie, but I care about my patients more than I care about some stupid legal issue."

"Stupid legal issue? Can you even comprehend how—?"

Valerie cut herself off when she realized that heads were poking out of rooms on either side of the corridor. She was alarming patients. This was neither the time nor the place to do this.

Valerie felt like boiling water was filling her up from the inside. She wanted to scream and shake Ella, to make her understand that the rules were important, but she couldn't do that here.

"My office, Ella. Now."

"Fine, but don't think you're going to get me to apologize. I'm not sorry."

Valerie growled under her breath and grabbed Ella's hand, practically dragging her toward the office.

All of the fragile self-control Valerie had tried to build up snapped in that moment. She pushed Ella ahead of her into the office and slammed the door shut behind them.

The moment the door was closed, she spun around and grabbed Ella, pinning her to the wall and kissing her hard. Ella squeaked in surprise, but after a moment she returned the kiss with equal fervor.

Valerie broke away from the kiss, slipping one hand immediately down into Ella's scrub pants, beneath her panties. She curled her fingers under and felt Ella's pussy which seemed to get wetter and more open for her instantly.

Ella had been driving her crazy for too long. Ella's eyes were dark blue and glazed with desire.

"If you can't behave, Ella, I'm going to make you behave." She pushed her fingers inside of Ella and Ella moaned, spreading her legs to give Valerie better access. "Do you want me to make you behave, Ella? Be careful how you respond, because if you say yes, I'm going to fuck you so hard that you won't be able to walk for days."

Valerie didn't know quite what had come over her. She felt insane with anger, lust, love and sexual desire all directed at Ella.

Ella moaned loudly at Valerie's words. "Yes," Ella gasped. "Please, I want it."

That was all the confirmation Valerie needed. She grabbed Ella and manhandled her over to the desk by her long wavy honey coloured hair, bending her over it and pulling her scrub pants and now damp white lace panties down to her knees.

She pushed her fingers back in Ella's pussy, curling them down towards her G Spot and started thrusting slow and deep.

She knew what Ella could take and she had every intention of giving her all of it. She added another finger and raised the pace a little. Ella's back arched, her ass rising temptingly, her moans got louder. God, fucking her was an exquisite pleasure. Taking her frustrations out on Ella's body seemed to be exactly what Valerie needed right now.

"You will learn to follow the rules, Ella. And I've got a new rule for today. You're going to come for me, but you're not going to touch your clit and neither am I. You're going to come from just my fingers inside you. Do you think you can do that?"

She punctuated her words with a twist of her fingers, pressing them hard into Ella's G-spot.

"Yes! Oh god yes, Valerie! If you keep doing that."

Ella rocked against the desk, no doubt getting some pressure against her clit that way, but Valerie didn't begrudge her that much. Ella started whimpering in frustration as she got closer, but she couldn't quite get there yet.

Valerie leaned down and whispered in her ear as she added a fourth finger and opened Ella up more. "I'm going to stretch you wide open for me, Ella. I'm going to fuck you so hard you will forget your own name. I'm the one in charge here, Ella, and I'm telling you to come. Right now. Come for me, Ella."

Ella's moans got louder and her body responded.

Valerie moved faster and harder against Ella's G spot. Ella was so slippery and welcoming that half Valerie's hand was now inside of Ella. She smiled to herself.

This is so hot. If nothing else, I'll fuck her into submission.

Ella muffled her scream against the desk as she came, her pussy clenching around Valerie's hand and her knuckles tight with her grip on the edges of the desk. She squirted all over Valerie's suit pants, all over her own panties and scrub pants and all over the floor.

Mmmm. You might be the best fuck of my life, but I'm pretty confident I might be best fuck of your life too.

Valerie gave her three more firm thrusts upon which Ella called out and squirted again before she pulled out and patted Ella's ass.

"Well, now that you've been taught a lesson about the rules, I would say it's high time for an apology, wouldn't you?"

Ella stood up and turned her lovely face to Valerie, her make up smudged and her hair messy. Her eyes were bluey- green and aquamarine again. She nodded, grinning. "How ever can I make it up to you, Dr. Bush?"

"I'm glad you asked." Valerie took her own pants off and moved Ella aside so that she could sit on the desk, spreading her legs.

"On your knees. Make me come with your tongue."

Ella went to work at once, moving straight to her knees with her scrub pants and panties still pushed down, pushing Valerie's thighs further apart and licking Valerie's pussy with abandon.

Valerie could feel her own wetness seeping down her inner thighs. She didn't think she had ever been more turned on than she was in that moment.

Valerie moaned and leaned back on her elbows, spreading her legs wider.

She felt Ella's tongue teasing her clitoris, Ella's mouth sucking her labia before Ella's tongue teased her entrance and then pushed inside of her as far as it would reach.

Valerie arched up and wrapped her legs around Ella's head, pulling her in deeper. Ella kept her tongue inside Valerie for a few moments before pulling out and going back to her clit, and oh dear god, that was good. Valerie rocked against Ella's tongue, riding out the steady waves of pleasure that emanated from the point of contact.

Valerie found herself right up to the edge of an orgasm in no time at all. Ella simply had that effect on her in a way that other women never had. She had always been able to make Valerie come in record time, and now was no exception.

Valerie's legs clenched around Ella's head as she came hard, pulsing onto Ella's hot, wet tongue. Ella licked her through it until Valerie became oversensitive and was forced to push her head weakly away.

Fuck. I needed that so badly.

Valerie couldn't believe what she had just done. Well, she could believe it, she had wanted Ella so very badly and now she had taken her, and taken her own pleasure from Ella.

She wanted to lie there and recover, but mind-blowing orgasm or not, she remembered she was still mad at Ella for breaking the rules yet again. She couldn't believe Ella had done that surgery.

Valerie forced herself to sit up and close her legs. "That will be all, Ella. You may go." She tried her best to look dignified, but she suspected that half-naked and still flushed from her orgasm was not the most dignified look in the world.

Ella gave her an indignant look and stalked out without a word.

For a few minutes, Valerie felt immensely satisfied, but as she caught her breath, cold, hard reality started to set in.

What had she just done? Ella had a girlfriend, and Valerie had just participated in Ella's cheating.

She had practically coerced Ella into being unfaithful. Sure, Ella had said yes, but Valerie had put her in that position in the first place.

Valerie felt sick with herself. She had never been cheated on before, but she knew how heartbreaking it must be, and now, she was the cause of that happening to another person. As much as she automatically disliked Ella's girlfriend, Valerie knew that no one deserved that.

She would have to put even more effort than she had been into avoiding Ella. Clearly, Valerie couldn't control herself around Ella, and that was unacceptable. Ella seemed to have just as little control around Valerie, so while this was on Ella too, Valerie still felt dirty for participating in Ella's cheating.

She would get the nurses involved in helping her avoid Ella. Nurses were wizards and could do anything around here. She would have to come up with a good reason to give them for why she wanted to avoid Ella, but she was sure that if she could win them over to her side, they would be invaluable.

Of course, avoiding Ella wasn't a good long-term plan. Valerie would need to think of something better eventually, but for now, that was all she had. Hopefully over time, she would learn to resist Ella better.

She reminded herself once more that this was all against the rules, and rules saved lives. Those rules may even save her heart, because as Lily had pointed out, if she allowed herself to fall for Ella, she would get hurt eventually. One way or another.

No, it was better to stay away from Ella, for more reasons than one.

Then why did the decision feel like a shroud being pulled over her?

17

ELLA

"So? What happened next?"

Ella felt herself blushing. "Well, you know."

"I get the idea, but I want the details, Ella. You know I'm not getting any right now. The least you can do is let me live vicariously through you."

Ella couldn't help grinning. She loved how she and Kate had the kind of friendship that they could talk about this kind of thing. Even though their friendship had started from a failed date, it hadn't left any awkwardness between them. It felt natural being friends with Kate, as it had from when they first met on the train. Ella realized that although she could appreciate Kate was attractive, that she wasn't really attracted to her and that had been important.

It had become quite clear to Ella recently that it was older powerful women who did it for her, and one in particular.

Kate was fun and easy to be around and Ella realized she probably did need a friend in her life. Friends were important, right?

"Well, she took my pants off and fucked me hard with her fingers over the desk. Then she sat on the edge of the desk and made me get her off with my tongue. After that, she dismissed me like a naughty schoolgirl."

Kate frowned. "What an ass. She could at least have said thank you."

"She wasn't exactly pleased with me at the time."

"It sounds like you did the best possible thing for your patient. I don't see why she's so mad about that."

"Oh, you don't know Valerie. Surgery is her first love, but rules are a close second. Any rule breaking is almost as bad as murder to her."

"She sounds awful. I don't understand why you have feelings for her."

"I do not have *feelings* for her!"

Kate rolled her eyes. "Seriously? You go all starry-eyed every time you talk about her, even when she's pissing you off. You're in deep, Ella."

Ella wondered if Kate was right. She was pissed at Valerie, but that didn't mean that the other feelings just went away. Maybe Kate had a point.

Still, that didn't mean she was at all impressed with Valerie right now. Valerie had taken avoiding Ella to a whole new level. They had hidden it quite well from her, but Ella strongly suspected that the nurses were involved in helping Valerie make sure they didn't so much as catch a glimpse of each other.

"I don't like that she's avoiding me," Ella admitted. "Whatever else was between us, she was my best friend at one point. I know she doesn't want more, and I'm not willing to engage in sex without a real relationship, but that doesn't mean we can't be friends. There's no chance of that when she won't talk to me, though."

"She sounds like she has her own issues to work out. I don't think there's anything you can do except leave her to it."

"Yeah, I guess so. I—hang on."

Ella's pager started beeping loudly. She glanced at it and swore. "I'm sorry, but I have to go.

There's been a building collapse and all available doctors are being called to the site to help."

"Go, work your magic. We'll chat when you're back."

"Thanks, Kate."

Ella grabbed her coat and rushed out.

The first thing she noticed was that Valerie was on the transport bus. Of course, Valerie wouldn't put avoiding Ella above helping patients when she was so desperately needed. Ella listened carefully as Valerie briefed them.

"Alright, people, listen up. This is going to be a tough one. There are a lot of people trapped under the collapsed building. We need to be ready as the rescue crews pull them out. You all know the drill —triage anyone who needs it and then attend to the red tags first. Good luck."

The site of the accident was a nightmare. There was smoke and dust everywhere. People were screaming and running around, and rescue teams were pulling horribly injured people out of the rubble.

From that moment, everything was a blur. Ella

was soon covered in blood and dirt, her eyes streaming from the smoke and dust.

She was just triaging a patient with a sprained ankle and a few small grazes as green when she heard a faint shouting.

"Hello? Help, someone please, help us!"

Ella approached the rubble cautiously. "Hello?"

"Please, are you a doctor?"

"Yes, I am." She peered through a small gap in the broken pieces of the building and saw a young woman peering desperately back at her.

"Please, my daughter is trapped. There's a beam through her leg. She's bleeding badly."

"Can you take off your sweater and use it to put pressure on the wound? I'm getting the rescue team right now."

Ella didn't wait to hear the response. She was off running, grabbing the nearest search-and-rescue guy by the arm.

"I need your help! There's someone trapped here."

"Ma'am, there are a lot of people who are trap—"

"Just hurry up and get your ass over here!" Ella snapped, yanking hard on his wrist. He allowed her to drag him to the small hole where she could just see the mother putting pressure on her daughter's leg that was pumping blood. It looked like the femoral artery. The child couldn't be more than seven. Ella knew she needed to get in there immediately or the little girl would die.

"Get in there!" Ella gestured frantically at the hole, but the man wasn't moving.

"I can't."

"What do you mean, you can't?"

"Look at that beam. It's half-shattered. It'll collapse at any moment. This whole area is too unstable. I'll need to get a team to stabilize it before going in."

"So go do that."

"I will, but I should warn you, it'll take at least an hour."

"An *hour*? She needs help *now*! She will die!"

Valerie suddenly appeared next to Ella. "What's going on here?"

Ella had never been so glad to see her. Surely, Valerie would understand. "Valerie, tell this man that we have to get in there right now to help that child."

Valerie peered through the gap and turned to the rescue guy. "She's right. Get us in there now."

"I'm sorry, but that's not physically possible. It'll take at least an hour. You're not to go in there before that."

Ella expected Valerie to argue—surely, she would fight for the patient—but instead, Valerie turned to her. "I'm sorry, Ella."

They both knew that an hour would be far too long. That girl would be dead way before then.

"No fucking way! If you won't get in there, then I will!" Ella grabbed her bag of essentials and pulled the hair elastic from her wrist and tied her hair up. A little girl wasn't dying on her watch.

"Ella, don't you dare! You will get yourself killed!"

"I can't let her die, Valerie. I just can't."

Ella grabbed her medical bag and shoved it ahead of her, squeezing herself through the small hole in the rubble.

Behind her, Valerie cursed under her breath. "You're going to be the death of me, Ella."

Then she crawled in after her.

18

VALERIE

Valerie knew that it was risky, but every cell in her body was screaming that she couldn't let Ella go in there alone.

The tunnel through the rubble opened up into a small cavern. Ella was already working on the child's leg. Valerie went to join her, quickly assessing the situation.

"You hold, I'll work," she said shortly.

Ella nodded. "Agreed."

Brains didn't tend to bleed as much as hearts did, which meant that Valerie had more experience in working with arteries than Ella did and they were both aware of that.

"It's ok sweetheart. We will have you out of

here in no time." Ella's voice was chirpy and confident to the frightened child.

Valerie hoped they didn't lose her.

"What is your name?" Ella smiled at the girl.

"Jessica," she gasped. She was pale and faint from the pain. Ella pulled a bottle of morphine and a needle from her bag.

"Why don't you close your eyes for just a second and I'll give you something to stop the pain."

Ella took the Jessica's limp arm and started working to put a line in so she could give some morphine.

She drew up morphine in a syringe and gave it to Jessica while Valerie worked hard on her leg. It was a mess and she worked quickly to repair the main artery to her leg, and do what she could with the broken femur to stop her from bleeding out. She was also worried about Jessica losing the leg, but first things first, she had to keep her alive. She wasn't an orthopaedic surgeon and either way, Jessica would need to be in an OR to have her leg worked on properly. This was just to keep her alive and get her stable.

They worked well as a team. It was instinctive. Ella passed her the pads and bandages and splint she needed before she even asked for them. They were the best poor little Jessica could hope for in this terrifying situation. Both Jessica and her mom were watching Valerie work in hope. Ella continued to talk normally to them to try and keep them positive.

"Right, that is you stable." Valerie had splinted and bandaged the thigh. She hoped her work on the femoral artery would hold until the girl reached an OR, but unfortunately arteries weren't always as predictable as Valerie would like them to be. They carried a lot of blood at high pressure. Sometimes, however good a surgical repair was, the blood flow would burst it.

Valerie let out a long sigh of relief and turned to the terrified mother. "She's stable for now. She should be fine for an hour or so while the rescue crew digs us out."

The mother flung herself into Valerie's arms. "Thank you. Thank you for my baby."

As Valerie embraced the trembling woman, she couldn't bring herself to regret breaking the rules. More than ever, she understood Ella's perspective. If not for breaking the rules, this child would definitely be dead right now.

Her introspection was interrupted by a

rumbling noise, followed by the rubble beneath them shaking violently.

Valerie glanced up at the ceiling just in time to see a huge piece of cement plummeting downward—straight for her.

"Valerie, watch out!"

Valerie didn't have time to react. She was frozen as she saw her death hurtling toward her.

It didn't happen like she expected.

She felt a muffled thump as something warm landed on her, and then a larger, heavier thump, but there was no pain. Instead, there was a sharp cry and sudden wetness.

Valerie blinked through the dust and felt like her heart stopped as her eyes made sense of what she was seeing.

Ella had thrown her body across Valerie's, and the rubble had hit her instead. As Valerie watched, it broke and rolled harmlessly to the side. But it left a long metal rod behind, sticking right through Ella's chest.

Valerie realized that the sudden wetness she felt was blood. Ella was slumped over her, unconscious.

"Ella! Please, no, Ella! HELP! Someone help us!"

She heard the sounds of the rescue crew working on digging them out, but who knew how long that would take now. It could be hours, and Ella didn't have hours.

Valerie forcibly clamped her mouth shut. Screaming and panicking wouldn't do Ella any good. With the greatest effort it had ever taken, she pushed her feelings aside and focused on the patient in front of her.

It looked like the rod had pierced between Ella's ribs and into her back. That was certainly better than her heart and gave Valerie a bit of time. Not much, but hopefully it would be enough.

Valerie's first instinct was to remove the rod, but she knew that would be a fatal mistake. She grabbed some bandages and used them to put pressure on the wound. She put a line in to start giving Ella fluids, medication, and hopefully soon, blood. It was the best she could do for now, until they were dug out.

Ella! Ella! Please don't leave me. I love you. I'll do whatever it takes.

She didn't know how long it would take, now that there had been a further collapse, but there was nothing she could do except try to keep Ella stable until she could get her to the OR.

Valerie held her hand and squeezed it.

"I love you, Ella." Valerie sighed. She knew now. This was love. This was the real thing. "If we make it out of here, I promise you, we can be together for real. Fuck the stupid rules."

It seemed that the universe was looking kindly on her today, because the collapse had actually made the surrounding rubble more stable. Within twenty minutes, the rescue crew was able to get to them, and not a moment too soon. Ella was pale as a ghost and her hands were going cold as her body prioritized blood flow to her essential organs.

The rescue team cut the rod sticking out of Ella and Valerie carefully helped load her onto the stretcher.

The ride back to the hospital was a blur. Ella's breathing was harsh and labored as blood filled her lungs. Valerie had to do some quick work to insert a tube and drain the blood so that Ella could get enough oxygen to keep her alive until Valerie could operate.

"Out of my way!" Valerie ran with Ella's bed, not caring who she bowled over, her only thought to get Ella to the OR as fast as possible. People scattered before her and the OR team gathered around her, following her into what Valerie knew would be the most important surgery of her life. Valerie immediately went to scrub in.

"Alright, let's get this thing out of her. Be ready, because she's going to start bleeding as soon as it goes."

Two of the residents gripped the rod and carefully pulled it out of Ella's chest.

Valerie was there with her clamps, immediately tying off the arteries and starting to repair the damage in Ella's chest. Her heart was pounding in her chest and her breathing was almost as shallow as Ella's. She feared she might pass out, but she knew that if she did, Ella was as good as dead.

All the other cardio surgeons were at the site of the accident. She was all Ella had, and Valerie couldn't let her down.

As she worked, some of the blind panic left her. Ella had suffered a very serious injury, but she was young and healthy and Valerie was an exceptional surgeon. The fact that she was still alive at this point in the surgery meant there was a good chance she would make it.

Valerie didn't like to get her hopes up with

patients this badly injured, but with Ella, hope was all that was keeping her going.

The surgery took hours, but by the time it was done, Valerie was confident that she had done her very best work. It would be a long road to recovery, but Ella should be just fine.

It was only after Ella's chest was closed and she had been wheeled into recovery did it really hit Valerie.

Her knees collapsed and she fell to the floor as the realization came over her. If that surgery had failed... Valerie would have been broken.

It was too late to avoid a relationship with Ella to prevent herself from getting hurt if something happened to Ella. Somewhere along the way, she had fallen in love with Ella and there was no going back.

Valerie didn't want to live without Ella. Seeing her nearly die had made that much very clear to her. As much as it scared her, she wanted to give this thing between them a real shot.

Of course, that didn't mean that Ella would take her back. Valerie had put Ella through a lot of shit and there was no guarantee that she would forgive her.

There was still the issue of the rules, but that

seemed supremely unimportant right now. True, if they hadn't broken the rules, Ella wouldn't have been hurt in the first place, but if they hadn't broken the rules, Valerie would never have fallen in love with Ella, and she wouldn't trade that love for the world.

"Doctor Bush? Are you alright?"

Stephanie was crouching down in front of her, her face set in concern.

Valerie gave her a silly smile. "I'm good, Stephanie. I'm in love."

Stephanie rolled her eyes. "I know that. I think everyone except Ella knows that. Finally come around, have you?"

"Yeah. Yeah, I have. Do you think she'll take me back? I... I have a lot to apologize for."

"So apologize, then. Ella loves you, Valerie. She would forgive you anything."

"You really think so?"

"I know it."

Valerie's grin hurt her face as she exited the OR. Even the chaos around her couldn't dampen her spirits, though she had to force herself to stop smiling lest she look like a psychopath in front of the families, smiling in the face of their loved one's misfortune.

No matter how much death she saw, though, nothing could diminish the burning joy she felt. She loved Ella and she wanted to be with her. Now, she just needed to convince Ella to take her back.

19

ELLA

Ella was woken by an obnoxious beeping. She was all too familiar with that beeping, but she only usually heard it when she was at work, not at home. She was at home, wasn't she? She was certainly in a bed. It didn't feel like her bed, though.

Ella's eyes fluttered open and she took in the sterile white walls of the hospital room. It started coming back to her. The accident. Her and Valerie crawling into the rubble. The collapse and throwing herself on top of Valerie. Then... nothing.

She blinked as someone sitting by her bedside came into focus. Valerie. She was slumped in a chair next to Ella's bed, fast asleep. Ella's heart warmed to see her there. Despite her and Valerie's issues, Ella was glad to have her here.

She tried to sit up, only to be greeted by a sharp pain in her chest. She must have been badly hurt in the accident. She couldn't prevent a soft gasp of pain as she slumped back down onto the bed.

Valerie jerked upright at once. "Ella! You're awake! How are you feeling?"

Ella tried to shrug, but it hurt, so she stopped. "Honestly, I've been better. I'm alive, though, right? As long as I'm alive, we can work with the rest."

"That we can. You had a metal rod through your lung. You know as well as I do that it'll be a long recovery, but you can make it. You're the strongest person I know, Ella. I know you can do this. And I'll be with you every step of the way."

"You will?" Ella wondered how long this new attitude of Valerie's would last, once the shock of seeing her injured wore off.

"Is the girl from the rubble ok?" Ella asked, suddenly remembering. "Jessica?"

"Yes, she will be fine." Valerie smiled. "She's been in OR3 with Dr. Haven from Ortho. He said she will make a full recovery and he managed to save the leg. He said we did a great job out in the field."

Ella smiled, suddenly relieved. It was all worth it if the little girl was ok. She imagined her making a full recovery and running around again.

"We need to talk, Ella. Are you well enough for a serious conversation?"

"Yeah, I'm fine. My head feels pretty clear, at least."

"Ella... seeing you nearly die made a lot of things clear to me. I've been a fucking idiot. I was pushing you away because I was scared—scared of getting hurt. When I'm scared, I retreat to what I know, and rules are what I know. I was wrong, Ella. I know you have a girlfriend, but—"

"Wait, what?"

"Your new girlfriend, Ella. The pretty brunette who keeps having lunch with you."

"Kate? I mean, we went on one date, but that didn't work out. We get on well, but there is no spark there. Ever since then, we've been good friends."

"Really? You don't need to say that just to spare my feelings."

"I'm not. I really tried with the date, but I

couldn't go through with it. I only wanted you, Valerie."

Valerie reached out and took one of Ella's hands. "I only want you too, Ella. I'm in love with you and I want to be with you, if you'll have me. I'm so sorry for the way I treated you. Can you ever forgive me?"

Ella didn't even need to think about it. "Of course I forgive you, Valerie. I'm so in love with you it hurts. I'd forgive you anything. I just want to be with you. That's all I ever wanted—for you to give us a chance."

"That's what I want, too. I'm sorry it took me so long to realize it."

"You can stop apologizing. You've already done that, and I've forgiven you. Consider it done."

"I love you, Ella."

Valerie leaned forward. Her brown eyes were warm and loving. Ella felt dizzy with the thought of what her body had been through, that Valerie had clearly saved her life and now Valerie wanted to be with her.

Properly be with her.

Valerie loved her.

"I love you, too."

Valerie smiled warmly at her and leaned down

and kissed her gently. Her lips were soft and full of hope and possibility for the future.

Ella smiled. It might have taken her nearly dying for Valerie to wake up, but she could take that if it meant they would live happily ever after.

"Are you nervous?"

"Yes, Ella, I'm nervous," Valerie snapped. She immediately took a breath and softened her tone. "I'm sorry. I didn't mean to snap at you. I just... I've given people such a hard time about relationships in the workplace before. They're probably not going to be impressed that I'm changing the rules for my own convenience."

"It won't just be convenient for you. A number of people will be able to be public about their relationships when they weren't before, and it'll open the doors for many more happy relationships in the future. Only doctors and nurses can really understand what it's like to be a doctor or a nurse. It means that dating within the workplace is a good option for us."

"Yeah, but they still may be unhappy."

Ella raised an eyebrow. "Since when did you

care about your rules making anyone unhappy? I seem to recall many shouting matches between the two of us about your rules, and you never backed down."

Valerie grinned. "You're right. I shouldn't care so much."

She took Ella's hand and walked up the first few steps in the lobby, putting them slightly above the waiting crowd of doctors and nurses.

"Thank you everyone for coming. I just have one quick announcement to make. I'm reversing the rule about relationships in the workplace. From now on, you may date and love whoever you wish, regardless of whether you work with them."

Even though she had known it was coming and Valerie had assured Ella she would go through with it, Ella could still scarcely believe it had actually happened. Valerie had never reversed a rule in her life, and here she was, doing exactly that.

There was shocked silence as everyone stared at the two of them.

Valerie took a deep breath. "With that in mind, I have a second announcement to make. Ella and I are in love. We're in love and… and I want to marry her."

Ella's jaw dropped as Valerie went to one knee,

pulling a box out of her pocket. She opened it to reveal a sparkling gold and amethyst ring. "Ella, will you marry me?"

Ella's knees were weak as she held out a trembling hand. "Yes," she whispered. "Yes," she repeated in a louder voice. "Of course, yes!"

Valerie slid the ring onto Ella's finger and Ella grabbed her by the scrubs, hauling her to her feet and kissing her so enthusiastically that she almost sent them both tumbling to the floor.

Valerie managed to throw a leg out to stabilize them, clutching Ella's waist and kissing her back with equal fervor.

The silence around them was finally broken as the assembled crowd broke out into cheers. They were suddenly surrounded by friends and colleagues hugging them and offering their congratulations. Ella was laughing and kissing Valerie at every chance she could get.

She couldn't believe it. Of course, she wanted to marry Valerie, but she had always figured it would be too much of a commitment for Valerie, what with her fear of getting hurt.

Ella stared at the ring on her finger, entranced. It was a symbol of Valerie's utter commitment and devotion to her.

"Take the day off work, you two!" Dr. Roth encouraged them. "You both deserve it."

"I just got back to work!" Ella said indignantly. "I didn't struggle through six weeks of recovery to take off on my first day back."

Valerie leaned close and whispered in Ella's ear. "If you come home with me right now, I'll make it worth your while. I'll have you screaming so loudly as you come that people across the block will hear you."

The words sent a shiver through Ella's body. As much as she loved surgery, Valerie's proposition was even more inviting.

"Fine, we'll take the day off."

There were chuckles around them, and Ella had a feeling that everyone had a pretty good idea what Valerie had whispered to her. She decided that it didn't matter. They didn't have to hide anymore, and it felt good.

Valerie insisted on driving them home even though Ella had been cleared to drive. It still felt strange to call Valerie's place home, but Ella was getting used to it.

After she was released from the hospital, she never went back to her apartment, except to collect some things. She and Valerie didn't want to be apart from each other anymore and had immediately agreed to move in together.

Valerie lifted Ella up once they were inside and Ella wrapped her legs around Valerie's waist. It was a familiar position for them, and one Ella never got tired of. She had been to the gym with Valerie a few times but had quickly discovered that working out wasn't for her.

That wasn't to say she didn't like going, though. Watching Valerie get all hot and sweaty while flexing her muscles—the same muscles she used to lift Ella with such apparent ease—was sexy as hell.

Ella kissed Valerie deeply, moaning at the taste of her mouth. Valerie had a unique taste that Ella found difficult to describe, but she was addicted to it. She couldn't decide what tasted better between Valerie's mouth and her pussy, but it didn't matter. She got plenty of both, which was exactly how she liked it.

Valerie carried her through to the bedroom and laid her gently down on the bed before undressing Ella, then herself. She trailed a hand over the scar on Ella's chest.

"It's fine, Valerie. I'm fully recovered now, thanks to you. I'm not going to break."

"You know, I'm not so sure. Maybe we should test that theory."

"Well, you're the heart surgeon. You would know best. How should we test it, doctor?"

"I think we should test your stamina. How about we get you really out of breath and see how you handle it?"

"A stress test? Sure. But I should warn you, a certain someone has been dragging me to the gym every day of my recovery. I'm pretty fit by now. It'll take a lot to get me winded."

Valerie gave her a wicked grin. "I was hoping you'd say that. Lie back and don't you dare come, Ella. We're testing how your heart reacts to stress, remember? And for that, you need to be as tense as a drawn bow for me. Do you think you can do that?"

"Yes," Ella breathed, already spreading her legs. Valerie paused for a moment before going to her drawer and getting out her strap on. Ella was already breathing slightly harder than usual as she watched Valerie grab the strap on harness and slide it over her hips. There was a pouch for a vibrating bullet just above the base of the dildo and Valerie turned on a bullet and popped it in the little pouch. Ella knew it would hit her clit if the angle was right when the dildo penetrated her deeply.

"Are you wet for me?" Valerie asked, although Ella was sure she knew the answer.

"Oh, so wet," Ella responded. "Why don't you have a feel."

Ella shivered with excitement as Valerie leaned in to test for herself, running her hand through Ella's folds and humming slightly in approval at what she found. "No coming," she reminded Ella. "Stress test."

Ella was liking this game already.

Valerie positioned the dildo and slowly pressed inside Ella's pussy. Ella felt the sweet ecstasy of the penetration as it hit her G spot and then the next thing she felt was the vibrations at her clitoris. She loved this strap on. It was one they had selected together—a particularly powerful one with the perfect curve to reach the G-spot.

Ella reached and adjusted the bullet so it pressed perfectly against her clitoris, embracing the delicious vibrations. Just being like this would probably be enough to make her come, but then Valerie started thrusting, and Ella's world went white with blinding pleasure.

An inhuman noise was drawn from her throat

as Valerie started pumping into her. They were both soon breathing hard, and Ella felt her thighs tightening up at her impending orgasm.

"Valerie, I'm going to come!"

"Don't you dare come," Valerie growled.

Ella whimpered, desperately scrambling for control. It was hard when Valerie was hitting all the right spots both inside and outside. Valerie kept going, heedless to Ella's ever-louder cries of distress.

"Valerie," Ella whimpered urgently. "Valerie, please... please, Valerie!"

"No."

Ella groaned in despair as she felt her thighs tightening up regardless of her urgent pleas to the contrary.

"Valerie, I'm going to come! Fuck, I'm coming now!"

Valerie pulled out, leaving Ella empty and wanting. Her pussy clenched helplessly around the empty space where the dildo had been a few moments ago. Her hips bucked upward as she desperately tried to get some relief, but there was nothing.

"Valerie, please," Ella whispered, her chest

heaving as she gasped, trying to get her breath back. "I need to come. I'm going to die if I don't."

"Now, Doctor Ashton, you should know better than that. Do I need to send you on a remedial course on basic medicine?"

"I don't care, as long as you make me come right now!"

"Oh, I will make you come, but not yet. We're going to wait until you calm down, and then we're going to stress test your heart again."

"Fuck my heart!"

"I beg to differ."

Ella was about to protest more, but then Valerie kissed her, and all protests vanished from her mind. She pressed herself up against Valerie, and the next thing she knew, Valerie was caressing her breasts.

This was hardly helping Ella calm down, but she definitely wasn't complaining.

Valerie's hands were gentle but firm on her nipples and she reached down to do the same thing, enjoying the feeling of pebbled flesh against her fingertips.

All too soon, Valerie was pulling away from her, but she didn't leave Ella wanting for long. She guided the slick dildo back into Ella's pussy and started fucking her once more.

This time, Ella got right up the edge even faster than the last time.

"Valerie! I need to come right now!"

Valerie responded by pulling out again. Ella felt like she might cry. Her body was screaming at her, but when she reached down for her clit, Valerie captured her wrist and kissed her palm.

"Not yet, my love. You can last a little bit longer for me, can't you?"

Ella found herself nodding. When had she ever been able to deny Valerie anything?

They made out some more before Valerie finally judged her ready enough to receive the dildo again. The touch of Valerie's lips and tongue was hardly less torturous than the dildo, but Ella didn't have the breath to point that out.

When Valerie finally entered her again, it only took two strokes before Ella was in dire straits.

"Please, Valerie!"

"You can hold it for me, my love."

"I can't! I'm going to come, Valerie! Oh fuck, please can I come, Valerie."

"Yes."

Ella screamed as she came on the next thrust.

Her whole world blanked out, overwhelmed by the pleasure that seemed to rip the very fabric of her being. It was so intense that it felt like it must surely have destroyed her, but when she came down, she was whole—sweaty and exhausted, but whole and wholly sated.

Valerie flopped down beside her, also catching her breath. "Come here. I want you to come on my tongue."

"There's no need," Valerie said faintly.

"There's no—did you come just from fucking me?"

Valerie nodded dazedly. "You were amazing, Ella. And the back of the vibrating dildo was pressing against my clit at the apex of every thrust. It's not surprising that I came."

"I guess not," Ella chuckled. "Come here anyway."

Valerie rolled closer and wrapped Ella easily into her arms.

"So, Doctor, is my heart strong enough?"

"You know, I'm still not one hundred percent certain. I say we give it half an hour or so, then test it again, just to be safe."

"Well, you know the rules of recovery better

than I do, Doctor, and I wouldn't want to break the rules."

"Say that again, will you? I want to record it."

"You wish."

Valerie was still laughing as Ella pulled her in for another kiss.

EPILOGUE
VALERIE -THREE YEARS LATER

"I can't believe she's really ours."

"She's not ours yet, not until the adoption papers have been officially stamped by social services. Those are the rules."

Ella rolled her eyes. "Rose has signed. We've signed. Social services have agreed that it's a good match. The rest is just red tape."

"Nevertheless, she's not ours yet."

"Semantics."

"Rules." It was a discussion they'd had many times before, but unlike in the early days of them knowing each other, the tone was teasing rather than angry.

"Yeah, yeah, I know you love your rules, babe.

Ours or not, I still want to hold her."

Valerie nodded. "Agreed."

They walked hand in hand through the hospital from the cafeteria back up the maternity ward. Rose brightened when she saw them. "Valerie, Ella! The nurses just brought her back from her checkup with the doctor. Everything looks good. She's perfect."

Though she was itching to hold Nikita, Valerie directed her gaze to Rose first. "How are you doing, Rose?" She handed Rose the blueberry muffin they had been sent to fetch, which Rose shoveled into her mouth at once.

"A little sore, but they gave me some good medication. I... I spoke to my parents. Now that I've had the baby, they're willing to take me back."

Ella squeezed Rose's hand. "That's great news, Rose. You know that you're always welcome back at our place whenever you want."

When she had become pregnant at fourteen, Rose's parents had kicked her out. She'd been brought into the ER for what the paramedics worried was a heart attack but turned out to be a panic attack. Valerie had been paged and had spent time talking to Rose.

She had quickly bonded with her and

convinced Ella to meet her. It didn't take much convincing to get Ella to agree to take Rose in. A few weeks later, Valerie had broached the subject of what Rose wanted to do with the baby. When she had told them she wanted to give it up for adoption, the way forward seemed clear.

Valerie and Ella had been talking about adopting for months now, and this was the perfect situation for it. They had made sure Rose had gotten the best possible medical care during her pregnancy, and Valerie was fully ready to keep taking care of Rose as a second daughter, but she knew that Rose missed her real parents and was glad that she would get a chance to renew that relationship.

"Thanks, Ella. I can't thank you enough for what you guys have done with me. I'm sure I'll still see you really often... if you're still okay with me visiting Nikita, that is."

"Of course we are," Valerie said warmly. "If you want to be a part of Nikita's life, then that's what we want, too. It'll be so good for her to know her birth mother, I think. We've been reading about adoption, and most adopted children want to meet their birth parents at some point. Knowing where you come from is important to everyone."

She and Ella had been nervous during Rose's long labor. Not about the baby—the labor was long, but standard, and Rose was completely healthy. No, they had worried that Rose might change her mind. That, apparently, was one of the major pitfalls of adopting a newborn. The birth mother had twenty-four hours in which to change their mind about the adoption. And they couldn't have blamed her if she did. Valerie knew, and had told Rose the same, that if she wanted to keep Nikita, they would still support her to be able to keep her. They were happy to keep Rose too.

Nikita was perfect; it was difficult to imagine Rose not changing her mind. But while Rose clearly loved Nikita already, she was still a child herself and she was adamant she wanted Valerie and Ella to be Nikita's parents. She wanted to have Nikita in her life as a little sister, but at fourteen, she wasn't ready to be her mom.

"I'm okay, really. Go on, you can hold her."

Valerie squeezed Rose's hand before turning eagerly to Nikita. Her daughter. She let Ella go to the crib first, picking her up and cradling her against her chest. Nikita stirred and started crying.

"What's wrong with her?" Rose asked immediately.

"Don't worry," Valerie soothed. "She's probably just hungry. Did you manage to pump?"

"Yeah, a little bit, one of the nurses helped me with it. I don't mind doing it- I want her to have it. It's in the fridge by the nurses' station, along with the donated milk. You can mix it. I think there's a microwave there too."

"I'll go get it."

By the time Valerie got back, Nikita was truly wailing, but she calmed down the moment Valerie offered her the bottle. Her little mouth sucking on the tip was the most beautiful thing Valerie had ever seen.

Once she was fed, Ella handed her over to Valerie, who finally held her daughter close to her chest. Nikita was sleeping peacefully now. Valerie's heart was so full, she felt like it might explode. She went to sit down with Nikita in a chair opposite Rose's bed.

Valerie decided to broach the tricky subject. "Will your parents be okay with you still being a part of Nikita's life?"

Rose lifted her chin. "They had better, because if they're not, then they're not getting me back in their life. They're welcome to kick me out again; I'll just come back to live with you."

"I'd pay good money to see their faces," Ella chuckled. "Thinking they're leaving you with nothing only to have us pick you up and take you to live with us and our daughter. You will always be welcome to live with us, you know that, right?"

"Well, hopefully it won't come to that. They miss me as well, and they want to make things work."

"You deserve a good relationship with your parents, Rose. Valerie and I will help in whatever way we can. If you want us to try to talk to them, we can do that. If you ever want to call us just to talk, we'll be here. And if you do get kicked out again, or even if you simply want to spend the night with Nikita, our door is always open."

Rose blinked back tears. "Thank you. You're both like second mothers to me, and I know you're going to be amazing moms to Nikita. She is the luckiest baby alive."

Ella took Valerie's free hand. "You know, I think we will."

They stayed with Rose chatting and cuddling Nikita. They were about to leave when Valerie got a call.

"Hi, Valerie, it's Sarah. I've got good news. Your adoption papers are all stamped and signed. Nikita is officially your daughter. You can take her home whenever is convenient for you. I'll email through a copy of the papers now."

Valerie's heart swooped. "Thanks so much, Sarah. You've been amazing through all of this."

"It's what I do. Seeing babies and children go to good homes like yours is why I got into this business."

"Well, you're certainly talented at it. Thanks again."

Valerie grinned widely at Ella. "She's ours. Officially."

"Does that mean we can take her home?"

"It does."

Valerie looked to Rose. "Are you ok for us to take her, Rose? It is ok if you want more time with her? Or you want to wait until tomorrow when you get discharged and you can come with us and see her settle in?"

Rose nodded. There were tears in her eyes. "I promise you guys, I'm more than ok with it. I'm not crying because I'm sad. I'm crying because I'm happy for her and for you. I'd actually love to get some sleep tonight and I know for a fact that will be easier for me without her here. I love her. I always will. But you guys are her future. Please, take her."

Ella went to grab the car seat that they had been keeping in the car for just this eventuality.

They strapped little Nikita in - she looked so tiny in it. Tiny with a little screwed up face. Valerie wondered what she might look like one day- their daughter. She carried her to the nurses' station, where they checked her out of the hospital officially.

The drive home was short, and before long, Ella and Valerie were putting Nikita in her crib next to their own bed.

She was sleeping peacefully now, though Valerie knew it wouldn't be for long. She and Ella were fully prepared for several months of sleepless nights. They had both taken a year of maternity leave- they wanted to be able to give Nikita everything they had- there would be time in the future for plenty of saving lives.

They would probably hire a nanny at some point when they went back to work, but Valerie and Ella had decided to see how it went with Nikita before taking that step.

Valerie hoped that at some point, Rose's parents might want to meet their granddaughter.

She knew that was probably a long way off, but they had time.

Even though Nikita was right next to them, Valerie checked that the baby monitor was working half a dozen times before finally conceding that it wasn't faulty and joining Ella in bed.

Ella wrapped herself around Valerie, and Valerie settled happily into the embrace.

"I can't believe we're actually parents," Ella murmured. "I expected to be terrified, and I am, but mostly, I'm so in love—with you and with Nikita. I have the best family in the world."

Valerie nodded. "She really is perfect. As is my beautiful wife."

They fell asleep in each other's arms, only to be woken about an hour later by screaming. Thankfully, Nikita just wanted to be fed. Valerie took that turn, and Ella took the next one.

So far, so good. It was only in the early morning that things got truly challenging.

Nikita woke up screaming again. She drank from her bottle, but she wasn't satisfied with that. They burped her and changed her, but she kept wailing with what Valerie could swear was the same volume as a police siren.

"What's next on the checklist?" Ella called over Nikita's continued screams.

Valerie glanced at the list on the fridge, a list they would both no doubt have memorized before long. "Stroller outside."

They had both read multiple parenting manuals, and all of them agreed that babies loved going on walks. It was cold outside, but light enough for a walk. They bundled a struggling Nikita up in multiple layers before getting dressed themselves, putting her in the stroller and stepping outside.

It was like magic. Within five minutes, Nikita had calmed down completely, leaving them to enjoy a pleasant walk with their brand new daughter.

They stopped at a park bench, parking the stroller next to them. It was cold, and Valerie put an arm around Ella for warmth.

"I told you, babies follow certain rules."

"Yeah, right. That checklist won't always work, you mark my words."

Valerie winked at her. "We'll see."

Truthfully, if Nikita didn't follow the rules Valerie expected, Valerie would deal with it. Since being with Ella, Valerie had become a lot more relaxed about rules. She would always be a rule-follower, but she didn't have a complete meltdown every time someone broke a rule—and was even known to bend a rule or two herself on occasion.

For her part, Ella had settled into her role at the hospital and accepted that she had to be more of a team player if everyone there was going to work together and sticking to the rules was part of that.

She and Valerie had negotiated on a number of rules that Ella found outdated or unreasonable. Some, Valerie wouldn't budge on. Others, she had reluctantly agreed that Ella had a point about. Together, they had come up with a system of rules that worked better not only for the two of them, but for everyone at the hospital.

Now, when Ella broke a rule, Valerie was more inclined to roll her eyes and make Ella get her off under the desk as punishment than shout. Ella, on the other hand, was much more likely to talk to Valerie before going completely off script and see if they could come to some kind of compromise.

There were days when they still got on each other's nerves, but those days were few and far between, and they always kept uppermost in their minds that they loved each other. That was more important than anything else.

"Do you think she'll be like me or like you? A rule follower or a rebel?"

"Did you hear that wailing earlier? There's no question that she'll be like you—a rebel all the way."

Ella chuckled. "I don't know about that. She did obey your checklist. Maybe she'll be like you after all."

"Or maybe she'll be a mixture of both of us. I think that would be perfect. We're both opposite extremes, and we balance each other out nicely. Hopefully, our daughter can embody that."

Ella squeezed Valerie's waist. "That's a perfect way to look at it, I think."

They were quiet for a few minutes, each lost in their own thoughts.

"Do you really think Rose's parents will be okay with the whole Nikita situation?" Ella asked after a while.

"I don't know. The fact that they kicked her out just for getting pregnant doesn't exactly give me much faith in them, but people do change. Maybe they really did miss her and love her enough to learn to be flexible."

"You'd know all about that. There was a time I thought you'd never budge on your stance on rules. I'm proud of you for evolving. It's not something everyone can do."

"I'm proud of you too, Ella. I know conforming doesn't come naturally to you, but you've done a remarkably good job of sticking to the rules we agreed on, even when they went against the grain for you."

"Your rules have saved lives, I'll admit that much, even though I don't agree with all of them."

"We don't have to agree on everything, my love. All we need to agree on is that we love each other, and we love our daughter. The rest, we can figure out from there."

"Yeah. Yeah, we can."

They took Nikita home shortly after that, not wanting her to catch a chill in this cold. She took another bottle while half asleep and then Valerie and Ella tucked her into bed.

Once they were sure she was settled, they returned to their own bed and snuggled under the covers together. Valerie felt sleep tugging at the edges of her consciousness but fought it.

"I love you," she mumbled.

"Love you too." Ella's voice was slurred in half-sleep, making Valerie smile tenderly.

Having said what she wanted to say, she let

FREE BOOK

I really hope you enjoyed this story. I loved writing it.

I'd love for you to get my FREE book- Her Boss- by joining my mailing list. Just click on the following link or type into your web browser: https://BookHip.com/MNVVPBP

Meg has had a huge crush on her hot older boss for some time now. Could it be possible that her crush is reciprocated? https://BookHip.com/MNVVPBP

ALSO BY EMILY HAYES

If you liked this one, please check out the next book in the Hearts Medical Series- A Heart of Hope

Can she find a way to lower the walls around her fiercely guarded heart?

This is an Age Gap, Ice Queen, Boss/Employee, Medical Sapphic/Lesbian Romance

Haunted by the grief of losing her beloved wife, Dr. Agnes Frame has no interest in love.

She is shocked when she finds an intense attraction to Cora, the new trauma surgeon. Agnes tries to deny the chemistry between them.

Will she ever be able to process her own feelings and give herself a second chance at love?

mybook.to/Hearts2

Printed in Dunstable, United Kingdom